NIM AT SEA

Also by Wendy Orr

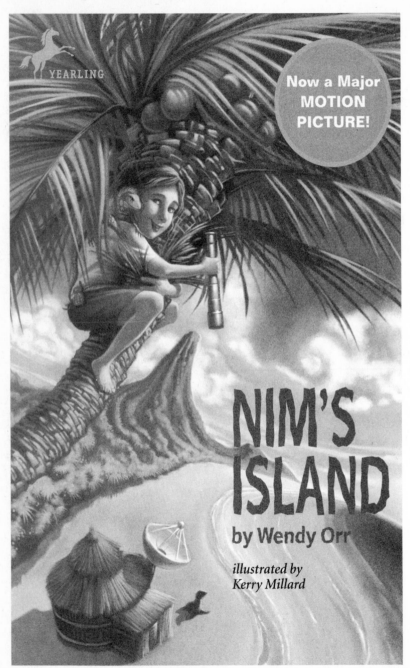

WENDY ORR
NIM AT SEA

Illustrated by
KERRY MILLARD

Alfred A. Knopf
NEW YORK

THIS IS A BORZOI BOOK PUBLISHED BY ALFRED A. KNOPF

Published in the United States by Alfred A. Knopf, an imprint of Random House Children's Books, a division of
Random House, Inc., New York. Originally published in Australia by Allen & Unwin in 2007.

Knopf, Borzoi Books, and the colophon are registered trademarks of Random House, Inc.

www.randomhouse.com/kids

Educators and librarians, for a variety of teaching tools, visit us at www.randomhouse.com/teachers

Library of Congress Cataloging-in-Publication Data is available upon request.
ISBN 978-0-440-42232-7 (trade)—ISBN 978-0-385-90535-0 (lib. bdg.)

Printed in the United States of America
March 2008
10 9 8 7 6 5 4 3 2 1
First American Edition

For Paula, who believed in Nim

Prologue

Long ago, when Nim was a baby, she'd had both a mother and a dad. Then one day, her mother had decided to investigate the contents of a blue whale's stomach. It was an interesting experiment that no one had done for thousands of years, and Nim's dad, Jack, said that it would have been all right, it should have been safe—but the Troppo Tourists came to make a film of it, shouting and racing their huge pink-and-purple boat around Nim's mother and the whale. The whale panicked and dived so deep that no one ever knew where or when he came back up again.

Nim's mother never came back up at all.

So Jack packed his baby onto his boat and sailed round and round the world—and finally, when the baby had grown into a very little girl, he found the perfect island where he could do his science and Nim could grow, wild and free like the animals they lived with.

The island has white-shell beaches, pale gold sand, and tumbled black rocks. It has a fiery mountain with green rainforest on the high slopes and grasslands at the bottom. There is a pool of fresh water to drink, a waterfall to slide down, and the hut that Jack built in a hidden hollow where the grasslands meet the beach. And around it, there's a maze of reef guarding the island from everything but the smallest boats, so Jack knows the Troppo Tourists or anyone else can never find their island.

But one day, Jack and his boat got lost in a storm—and Nim was left alone on the island, until her e-mail friend Alex Rover, the most famous and cowardly adventure writer in

the whole world, crossed the sea to rescue her. And then
Nim's most secret wish came true: Jack came floating back—
and Alex stayed.

IN A PALM TREE, on an island, in the middle of the wide blue sea, is a girl.

Nim's hair is wild, her eyes are bright, and around her neck she wears three cords. One is for a spyglass, one is for a whorly, whistling shell, and the other holds a fat red pocketknife in a sheath.

With the spyglass at her eye, Nim watched the little red seaplane depart. It sailed out through the reef to the deeper dark ocean, bumping across the waves till it was tossed into the bright blue sky. Then it rose so high and so far it was nothing but a speck, and floated out of sight.

"Alex is gone," Nim told Fred.

Fred stared at the coconuts clustered on the trunk.

Fred is an iguana, spiky as a dragon, with a cheerful snub nose. He was sitting on Nim's shoulder, and he cared more about coconuts than he did about saying goodbye. (Marine iguanas don't eat coconut, but no one has ever told Fred.)

As Nim threw three ripe coconuts *thump!* into the sand, she remembered Alex saying, "I never knew anything could taste better than coffee!" the first time Nim opened a coconut for her.

Nim looked down at her father, sitting like a stone on Selkie's Rock. Jack's head was bowed and his shoulders slumped. Nim had never seen him look so sad.

And suddenly she knew she'd made a terrible, terrible mistake.

The mistake began when she answered Alex's very first e-mail, back when she'd thought that the famous Alex Rover was a man and a brave adventurer like the hero in the books "he" wrote. That led to Alex's ending up on the island—and when she did, Jack and Nim wanted her never to leave. Sometimes it felt good to be three instead of two.

But other times Nim wanted Jack just for herself, the way it used to be. Or she wanted Alex just for herself, because Alex was *her* friend before she was Jack's. Sometimes, when Alex and Jack told Nim to go to sleep while they talked late into the night, Nim felt left out and lonely.

Then, earlier this morning, the little red seaplane had arrived, bringing all the things that Alex had asked her editor back in the city to send. It was the first time a plane had ever landed on Nim's island. Nim could tell that Jack was worried that the pilot would notice how beautiful the island was and would want to come back again and again.

Whenever Jack was worried, Nim was too. And when Nim was worried, so were her friends Selkie and Fred. (Selkie is a sea lion who sometimes forgets that Nim is a girl and not a little sea lion pup to be looked after and *whuffle*d over.) They both stuck close to Nim every time she walked back and forth between the plane and the hut.

"I've never seen animals do that before!" exclaimed the pilot.

Nim didn't know what to say, partly because she didn't know exactly what he hadn't seen before, and partly because she'd never spoken to any person besides Jack and Alex. She grabbed a crate and opened it up. Inside there were books! Thin books and fat, short books and tall, history and science books, mysteries, adventures, and more and more and more! Nim started to look through one when—

"Come on, Nim!" said Alex. "There'll be time to read when everything's off the plane."

The pilot pulled out two big solar panels. "Great!" Jack exclaimed, because he wanted them for the new room he planned to add to the hut—one created especially for Alex to write her books in. Jack balanced the panels on his head and walked very slowly and carefully up toward the hut.

"Who's going to take this one?" the pilot asked, pointing to a crate.

Nim stepped forward eagerly. But just as she was about to

reach for the crate, the pilot handed it to Alex. First Alex stumbled, then she tripped, then *crash!* the crate fell with a tinkle of broken glass.

"Oh, *no!*" Alex wailed. "What have I done?"

"Jack's test tubes!" Nim shouted. "You should have let me take it!"

"I was trying to help!"

"But I didn't need help! You just got in the way!"

"I'm always in the way these days!" Alex snapped. "Maybe you and Jack would be better off without me."

"I think we would!" Nim shouted, and stomped off without waiting for an answer.

She's right! Alex thought. *Nim and Jack lived here perfectly happily all those years without anyone else—they don't really need me. Nim's been cross with me a lot lately and I've never seen Jack be so worried. I think . . . I think I'm changing their lives too much. What if they've secretly been wanting their old lives back— and just haven't wanted to say so?*

Alex understood about being afraid to say so. Before she came to the island, she was so afraid of saying anything to anyone that she hardly ever left her apartment. She was a famous person, but only through her books. Her life had totally changed since she flew across the world to find Nim.

"Last one!" The pilot handed her a large envelope. "And now, time for me to go."

Alex opened it. She pulled out the letter and stared at it without reading.

"Wait! Can I . . . can I go with you?"

"Sure!" said the pilot. "But don't you need to pack?"

Alex knew that if she saw Jack or Nim she would never be able to leave, even if it was the right thing to do. "No," she said, "I'm ready to go."

Alex Rover climbed into the little red seaplane. And was gone.

Hours later, Nim scrambled down from the coconut palm and buried her face in Selkie's warm neck, because the sea lion loved her no matter how bad Nim was—and the feeling in Nim's stomach told her this was the very worst thing she'd ever done.

Jack loved her too, but Nim didn't know if he still would when he realized it was Nim who had chased Alex away.

"Meet me at the Emergency Cave," she told Selkie, because suddenly the sun and sea were shining much too bright.

Not to Scale

Emergency Cave

Fire Mountain

Winds

Rainforest

Pool

Tabletop Garden

Frigate Bird Cliffs

Only the deepest, darkest cave could match the way she felt inside.

Selkie gave a disapproving sort of *hrumph* and lolloped down to the sea. Nim and Fred headed inland, toward the bottom of Fire Mountain, past the Hissing Stones, and across the Black Rocks.

Scrambling up the boulders was good because it was such hard work Nim couldn't think about anything else. But when she got to the cave, she remembered: Alex telling her stories when they were trying to sleep on the hard cave floor, Alex watching the sunrise on the very first morning, Alex crying when Nim skinned her knee.

Nim crawled into the deepest corner of the cave to be as sad and alone as she could possibly be. She hiccuped and coughed and cried and blew her nose, then dropped her hanky.

It was when she was feeling around in the dark for her soggy hanky that she found the map.

Alex had drawn the map when she told one of her stories. It showed an island that was part of a city with even bigger parts next to it. It was as different from Nim's island as anywhere could possibly be.

It was the place where Alex's books were published, in a tall, shining building whose top floors were up above the clouds. It was where Alex's editor worked—the one who'd sent the supply plane.

Nim stuffed the map into her deepest pocket and started crying all over again. She cried so hard that Selkie pulled herself all the way up from the sea to the cave to comfort her. But when Nim wouldn't stop crying, no matter how much Selkie *whuffled* and *snuffled*, Selkie went just outside the cave entrance so that she could do tricks to make her friend smile. She balanced a rock on her nose, then threw it up in the air and off the cliff. She sat up high on her tail and flapped her flippers as if she were trying to fly. She did a handstand on her front flippers. She went through all her tricks over and over and barked at Nim in between to make her stop crying.

Finally Selkie showed Nim her best trick ever—a handstand right on the edge of the rocks, then a flip into a perfect dive all the way down to the water.

It was a long way down, and it was a very good trick—but Nim wouldn't come out to see.

And so Nim also didn't see the giant cruise ship that had come around the point and anchored not far from the cliffs.

She didn't see the inflatable motorboat with people snorkeling around it, or the second motorboat chugging quietly out from the other side of the ship. She didn't see the man watching the sea lion do her tricks lift his rifle and shoot Selkie with a tranquilizer dart. She didn't see him instruct his crew to heave Selkie into his boat and speed away with her to their ship.

But Fred did.

Fred *had* been watching Selkie and hoping she'd do his favorite flipping-a-coconut-high-off-the-cliffs-*smash!*-onto-the-rocks trick. When she did the handstand-dive, he ran to the edge of the cliff to see if she'd smashed a coconut on her way down.

What he saw made Fred forget all about coconuts.

First he scrambled down, then he scrambled back up. Then he rushed into the cave and head-butted Nim's leg. When she still didn't pay attention, he climbed onto her shoulder and sneezed his cool saltwater spray in her face.

"Yuck, Fred!" said Nim. But when Fred scurried to the edge of the cliff, Nim followed.

The boat was chugging back to the ship. Through her spyglass Nim could see Selkie at the bottom of the boat.

"They've killed her!" Nim screamed.

But then Selkie lifted her head, and Nim saw the men tying ropes and nets around her.

She had to save her friend! Fast!

Fred scrambled to her shoulder and clung on tight. Nim stood on the edge of the cliff. The water was a long way down.

What if I hit the rocks? Nim thought.

She jumped, as high and far as she could, and twisted into a dive.

She hit the water.

Nim's lungs were bursting and her ears were hurting. But soon she saw light above her head, and kicked and spluttered her way up to the air.

The boat was already a long way out, and the waves were strong on this side of the island, but Nim had no choice. She took another deep breath and began to swim with all her might.

2

JACK SAT ON SELKIE'S ROCK for a long, long time, staring out at the empty sky. He felt as if a part of his world had vanished with Alex's plane and he'd been left behind.

He reread the letter he'd found on the beach.

Dear Alex,

I'm glad the materials I organized for the supply ship were useful; I hope these things will all be too. I guess that new cabin must be just about finished by now and you've all got clothes to wear again. It was quite amusing to read about your banana-leaf dress in your first e-mail!

Your apartment and furniture have been sold, as per your instructions. I'm enclosing all the paperwork. However, just in case you change your mind about staying on that little island forever, I'm also enclosing a new passport and credit card to replace the ones you lost.

Now, enclosed please find the reason I've been so busy: the first copy of your new book! I am very proud to be the editor of this book: I think it's wonderful, and we're going all out to make sure it'll be your biggest bestseller.

Please let me know if there's anything else I can do.

Yours,

Delia Defoe

"Why would she . . . ?" said Jack. But no matter how many times he read the letter, it still didn't explain why Alex had gone.

"What could have suddenly made her so unhappy?" he asked the sea. "Did the things on the plane remind her of what she'd been missing? Did she suddenly want to go and be famous again? And why couldn't she tell me?"

But the sea didn't answer, and it didn't matter what Jack wondered, because Alex was gone—and soon he'd have to tell Nim, which would be almost worse than knowing it himself.

Jack had seen Nim's face when she'd opened that big crate of books. He knew she'd be lying somewhere, her head on Selkie's back and Fred curled on her stomach, lost in a story, not even realizing everything had changed.

Meanwhile, Alex sat in the passenger seat of the seaplane, too frozen with sadness to even be afraid. She looked back at the gold sand of Turtle Beach, the light clear blue of Keyhole Cove, the palm tree Nim always climbed, and the shack they'd just built, and she wondered if she had made a terrible mistake.

Then she thought about what Nim had said, and knew she cared too much about her friends to stay if Nim didn't want her.

Fred jumped off Nim's shoulder when they hit the water, but he stayed under only long enough to grab one big mouthful of seaweed before popping out beside her.

Selkie was part of Fred's life, and Fred wanted her back.

They were both swimming as fast as they could, straight out to sea, but the boat was pulling away even faster. Nim's heart was pounding; it hurt when she breathed and she was swallowing too much water.

I . . . huff . . . can't . . . go . . . huff . . . fast enough! she thought. She rolled onto her back. Fred kept on gliding under the water just beside her.

When Nim had caught her breath and rolled over again, the cruise ship was getting closer—but the motorboat with Selkie and the seal-nappers had disappeared.

It can't have gone! Nim thought. *It must be on the other side of the ship.*

That was when she saw the huge pink-and-purple name on the ship's bow: THE TROPPO TOURIST, the company that Nim was more afraid of than anything in the world.

Nim tried to swim faster, but it didn't take long before she was gasping, swallowing water and spitting it out again. She rolled onto her back; her arms whirred, her legs kicked . . . and her head knocked hard against a rubber boat.

Hands grabbed her arms. A man and a woman, with horrified faces and matching pink-and-purple T-shirts, stared down at her.

"Fred!" screamed Nim.

Fred scrabbled to her shoulder, and they were hauled into an inflatable motorboat like the one that had seal-napped Selkie.

"You said you'd counted, Kelvin!" shouted the woman, whose T-shirt said I'M KYLIE.

"I did!" Kelvin answered. "There were fifteen kids in that snorkeling group and we took fifteen back . . . I think."

"If you'd counted," Kylie insisted, "we wouldn't be fishing this poor kid out of the water now!"

"Maybe she's a castaway from that deserted island: Kid Crusoe!"

Nim didn't have enough breath to say her name was Nim Rusoe, not Kid Crusoe.

"Where were you heading to, honey?"

"To the boat," Nim whispered.

"Just in time," said Kelvin. "We're about to set sail."

Nim still couldn't see the other little boat. All she could see was the cruise ship: its white length stretching forever in front of her, and its towering decks reaching to the sky.

It was the only place Selkie's boat could have come from, and the only place it could have gone. If Nim was going to rescue Selkie, she had to get on the ship.

Fred sneezed.

"What *is* that?" Kelvin asked.

Fred clung tight to Nim and glared his fiercest dragon glare. "He's my friend," Nim explained.

"If you say so!" Kelvin grinned. He didn't look as if he really wanted to touch Fred anyway.

"Not to worry, you can keep your, er, pet," said Kylie.

"She's delirious," Kelvin whispered.

"Hey, where's your snorkel?" asked Kylie.

"I don't know," said Nim.

"Never mind," said Kylie, with a big anxious smile. "We won't tell anyone you lost a valuable snorkel if you don't tell anyone you nearly missed the boat."

"Great idea!" said Kelvin. "Look, kid, we don't want to get you into trouble. And wouldn't your parents be mad if they found out you hadn't stayed with the other kids the way you were supposed to?"

"You'd probably be grounded all the way to New York City!"

"Stuck in your cabin for six whole days—you wouldn't like that, would you?"

Nim felt as if her head was going to explode. "Where's *Selkie?*" she demanded.

"Who's Selkie?"

"We haven't lost another kid, have we?"

"She's a—" But Nim stopped just before she said "sea lion." She remembered the part in Alex's book when the hero tricked the bad guys out of kidnapping him because they thought he was crazy.

"She's a mermaid," said Nim.

"Poor thing! She's had too much sun!"

"Stayed too long in the water!"

"Wrap her up—grab that jacket."

Kelvin dropped a pink-and-purple Troppo jacket over Nim and Fred. He still didn't seem to want to touch Fred.

"Don't worry, kiddo," said Kylie. "I'll get you settled down before you see your parents. You'll be fine!"

The boat bumped against the ship. A long plank with rope railings led up from the water to a door halfway along the side. Kelvin grabbed a rope, and Nim and Fred followed Kylie up the ramp and onto the giant ship.

3

NIM FOUND HERSELF in a big open room with small palm trees and large, bright flowers. There were decks above her, a long hall lined with doors leading off to the left, and a white stone fountain to the right. And everywhere she looked there were people: sitting on the edge of the fountain, looking out over the rail, relaxing in deck chairs, perched at small tables with drinks and snacks, sitting at desks across from beaming *Troppo Tourist* crew members. They were talking and laughing and eating and gazing around.

Nim felt frozen, too stunned to even move.

"Are you okay?" Kylie asked worriedly.

Nim nodded, but in truth she could hardly breathe. She took a step closer to the fountain, where water bubbled and splashed from the mouth of a carved-stone dolphin. In the tiny pool around it were two dolphins swimming in endless circles.

Nim gasped. The dolphins she knew swam free and far across the sea—these animals barely had room to splash.

"This way," Kylie said, quickly steering Nim down a flight

of stairs and into another long hallway with a shiny green floor and walls lined with doors. There were no windows, and even though light shone from bright lamps in the ceiling, Nim felt as closed in as if she were in a cave. Fred curled himself tightly around her neck, peering out from under her chin.

Kylie pulled out a key, unlocked the door marked *12*, and ushered Nim into a cabin. There were two bunk beds, two sets of drawers, and a door into a tiny, shiny room. She reached in and handed Nim a towel.

"You'd better get warm and dry before you go back to the Kids' Klub," she said. "Were you supposed to have lunch with your mom and dad?"

"No," said Nim.

"Well, how about I get you something yummy? What about a hamburger and milkshake? I bet that'll make you feel better!"

"Maybe," said Nim.

Kylie tried to smile reassuringly. "You'll be fine, don't worry!" She stepped out the door, called, "Have a shower if you want to warm up!" and disappeared.

Fred crawled down from Nim's shoulder.

Nim waited a second, and tried to open the door.

Nim had lived all her life on the island. She'd read about locks, but she'd never seen one. She'd never known what it would be like to be inside a small room and not be able to get out. She pulled the knob and kicked the door as hard as she could.

"Ow!" she shouted, rubbing her big toe.

"Now what do we do?" she asked Fred.

Fred felt braver now that Kylie was gone. He decided to explore the cabin. In the tiny room behind the door he found an even tinier room with glass walls and a hard floor with a hole in the middle.

Alex had told Nim about toilets that flushed and showers like waterfalls that ran as hot or as cold as you liked. When Nim wanted to get clean, she swam in the sea or soaked in the Rainforest Pool. She turned the tap on—and the water gushed out just like Alex had said, warm as sunshine.

"I'll try it if you will!" she told Fred.

Nim stuck her arm under the spray, then her leg, and then she and Fred jumped back and forth under the water and out the door, till there were puddles on the floor, splashes up the walls, and drops on the ceiling. Fred got so hot he couldn't stay still, and raced crazily around the cabin and up and down the bunks till he was worn out. Nim turned the tap off, rubbed her hair with the towel, and shook herself to dry her clothes.

She was wearing a blue shirt and red pants made with the material brought by the supply ship. Jack had designed the pants with drawstring legs that could be pushed up into shorts for coolness or pulled down smooth for swimming or palm tree climbing. There were lots of pockets for Useful Things, including one extra-deep pocket with its own drawstring to keep special things safe. Nim pushed the legs up into shorts now, because they were soggy and dripping.

Everything else in the bathroom, and quite a lot of things in the cabin, were soggy too—especially the pillow Fred was stretched out on.

The door opened, and Kylie came in with a tray piled with food. Her face went pale when she saw the cabin. "I see you had a shower!" she exclaimed. "I bet you feel better now!"

"A little bit," Nim said.

"Well, this ought to fix you up. Look what I've brought you: milkshake, hamburger, chips, some Jell-O, cake, a banana, and a hot chocolate in case you're still cold."

"Thank you," said Nim. She stared at the food and wondered what to try first; the banana was the only thing she recognized. Nim put it in her pocket when Kylie wasn't looking.

"Those are interesting shorts you're wearing," Kylie said. "I thought they were a wetsuit."

"They're wet shorts," Nim explained. She opened the hamburger and found some lettuce. *Something else I know!* Nim thought, but Fred snatched it and gulped it down.

The milkshake slid cold down her throat, and then hot chocolate warmed it up again. Nim tried a mouthful of slippery green Jell-O. She liked the way it squished through her teeth. She ate a handful of salty, crunchy chips and the pickle from the hamburger. Fred sampled the food too. He liked the Jell-O best. Nim loved the hot chocolate. And the crunchy chips. It was hard to decide.

Kylie watched Nim and Fred trying the food, mouthful by mouthful. "That's an interesting way to eat," she said.

"It's interesting food," Nim said politely.

Suddenly there was a faint *rumble* from somewhere deep inside the ship, and the floor beneath Nim's bare feet began a steady, chugging tremble. The ship's engines had started.

If I don't get out of here soon, thought Nim, *it'll be too late to rescue Selkie and get back to the island!*

"Do you feel well enough to go back to the Kids' Klub?"

Nim nodded. She had to start looking for Selkie somewhere.

"Do you want to take that—I mean, your friend—with you?"

Fred rushed to the plate, slurped down the last of the Jell-O, and raced up to Nim's shoulder. Nim picked up the pink-and-purple jacket—maybe she could use it as a type of disguise? She threw it over Fred so he was disguised too, all except for his watching eyes and iguana grin.

They followed Kylie halfway down a hall to a fish tank with a sign saying PIRANHA DECK. Nim held Fred's tail to make extra sure he didn't fall in.

Kylie stopped and pressed a button on the wall opposite the tank. Doors slid open, and she ushered Nim and Fred into a small empty room. All that was in it was a doormat that said THURSDAY, a mirror on the wall that showed their frightened faces, and a row of buttons beside the door with a picture of an animal on each one. Kylie pressed the ARMADILLO button and the doors slid shut.

Nim knew about elevators: Alex had told her about her home, a building that was half as high as Fire Mountain, with elevators that took her up to her apartment and back down to street level with just a press of a button. What Nim didn't know was that the elevator would leave her stomach down at the bottom while it whisked the rest of her up to the top. Fred didn't know either. He was so surprised he sneezed his last mouthful of Jell-O all over Nim's neck.

"Yuck, Fred!" said Nim. It was the first completely true thing she'd said since she'd got on the ship.

"I bet your friends will be glad to see you," Kylie said as the elevator stopped.

The only friends Nim had ever had were Selkie and Fred, plus Chica the sea turtle and Galileo the frigate bird—but Chica came ashore only once a year to lay her eggs, and Galileo was only your friend if you had a fish in your hand. So for just a minute Nim thought, *Selkie's here!*

But when the elevator doors opened, the sign said AR-MADILLO DECK, and the cage beneath it held two little armadillos rolled into tight armor-plated balls.

Kylie turned, and Nim followed her toward a swimming pool. Selkie wasn't in it, or in the little pool with a spray that fountained up like the water through the rocks of her own Keyhole Cove. They walked on, past a door marked TROPPO TEENS, past another marked TROPPO TOTS, and then stopped at the KIDS' KLUB door.

Inside, some people were making things at tables, others were playing games on giant computer screens, some were running, and others were talking; some were bigger than Nim and some smaller. They were as crowded and noisy as seagulls on a beach—and, except for another pink-and-purple-

T-shirted woman, whose name tag said KRISTIE, they were all . . .

Kids! Nim thought. *I didn't think there'd be this many kids in a whole city!*

Kylie pushed her firmly into the room and pulled Kristie out the door. "Not quite right in the head," Nim heard her say. "She shouldn't have been allowed to go snorkeling—and look at the lizard she caught out there! We couldn't get it away from her."

"Never mind—the Professor can deal with that."

But Nim wasn't listening anymore.

In the books Nim had read, kids had adventures together; sometimes they were friends at the beginning of the story, and other times they fought and ended up friends in the end. *But how are you supposed to know what to do,* Nim wondered, *when you can't even figure out what they're doing—and they don't even notice you?*

She backed up against the wall and watched them as if they were a flock of birds that weren't used to her yet.

A girl in front of one of the giant computer screens stopped spinning her steering wheel and looked right at Nim. She smiled, and Nim tried to smile back. The girl came over.

"I'm Erin Caritas. Did you get on at that port two days ago too? I thought we were the only ones." She pointed to a slightly smaller dark-haired boy who was riding a strange sort of motorbike that kept bouncing him off the seat but didn't go anywhere. "That's my brother, Ben."

Fred stuck his head out from under the jacket and sneezed.

"Cool!" said Erin. "What's his name?"

Suddenly a bunch of kids were around them, so close Nim

could hardly breathe, asking questions so fast no one even noticed she wasn't answering.

"Where'd you get that thing?"

"Can I touch it?"

"What *is* it?"

"How come the Professor let you have it?"

Fred sneezed again, harder, and they jumped back.

Kristie came back inside and the kids turned to her.

"Look what the Professor gave her!"

"Of course!" Kristie exclaimed. "You must be the Professor's kid!"

Nim didn't know what a Professor's kid was, but she knew that it might be the disguise that would let her save Selkie.

"All right then, why don't you tell us about your little friend here."

"He's a marine iguana," Nim began. "He can swim and dive. . . ."

"Does he do tricks?"

"Show us some tricks!"

Nim thought fast. Fred could do lots of things. He could gulp down coconut so fast he wouldn't even notice a rare coconut pearl inside. He could play coconut soccer. He could sink like a stone to the bottom of Keyhole Cove. He could ride on Nim's shoulder and sneeze on her neck.

"Ladies and gentlemen!" Nim began, imitating Alex's best storytelling voice. "Allow me to present: *Fred!*"

Fred stuck his head out from behind her neck to see why she was calling him, saw all the people staring, and stared back even harder.

It wasn't exactly a trick, but: "Fred here is a champion

starer," said Nim. "He can stare hard enough to make anyone look away!"

"Not me!" said a red-haired boy. He came closer and stared into Fred's eyes. Fred stared back. The boy moved closer. Fred sneezed.

"Gross!" shouted the boy, and jumped back into the crowd.

Everyone laughed and clapped.

"Thank you, Fred!" said Nim. "What would you like to do for your next trick?"

Fred stared at her. His mouth opened and shut as if he were eating.

"I don't have any coconut," said Nim.

Fred brought his face right up to hers and stared harder.

Everyone laughed again. "Does he really understand?" asked a girl in a sunflower hat.

"No," said Kristie. "I went to the Professor's lecture on reptiles and he said they don't understand language."

"Is he really hungry?" Erin asked Nim.

"Fred's always hungry," said Nim.

Erin reached for a plate of fruit on a table and held out a segment of mandarin. Fred snatched it, started to gulp—and spat mashed mandarin across the room.

Kids jumped, yelled, and laughed. All except Erin, and Ben, who'd finally got off the jolting motorbike and was watching quietly. "I'm sorry, Fred!" Erin said, and gave him a kiwi fruit. Fred didn't like kiwi fruit either. Chomps of green mush flew across the room and everyone laughed harder.

Erin looked as if she was going to cry. "He likes strawberries," said Nim.

Erin offered a strawberry. Fred gulped it down—and didn't spit it out!

Everyone clapped.

"Fred has lots of other tricks," said Nim, "but he mostly does them with another performer. In fact, he needs to go rehearse with her now."

Fred settled himself back on her shoulder, and Nim marched out the door.

Oh, Selkie! she thought. *Where are you?*

4

JACK STILL HADN'T figured out what to say to Nim. *Let her be happy a little longer*, he decided, and went on staring out at the empty sea.

Alex was still frozen in her seat, clutching the envelope the pilot had handed her just before she'd jumped on board.

She knew it held the first copy of her new book, but she wasn't ready to see it. There was also a credit card, a passport, and a thick contract saying that her apartment and furniture had been sold. She'd asked Delia to do that, but she was surprised that there was no letter explaining it.

Just as she remembered that there *had* been a letter, which was probably float-ing in the water at the island now, the little red seaplane bumped gently down onto the waves and pulled up beside the Sunshine Is-land wharf. Alex wiped her eyes and climbed out.

37

It was three months since she'd landed here on her way to rescue Nim. She'd been nervous then, afraid of flying, afraid of crowds, afraid of the sea—but it had been exciting too, because she'd been turning into someone new. But now that Nim didn't want her on the island anymore, there was nothing to do but go home.

Except that she no longer had a home.

You still have to go somewhere! she told herself.

"Can you take me to the airport on Isla Grande when you've refueled?" she asked the pilot.

He shook his head.

"I'm afraid my old plane needs a complete service after such a long flight. It'll be too dark before I'm finished—and I'm not a brave adventurer like you, Alex Rover! My seaplane and I don't fly at night."

"How about in the morning?"

"I'm going on holiday," the pilot said. "I'd have left already if Delia Defoe hadn't talked me into doing your supply drop first."

"Okay," said Alex. "I guess I'll have to find the pilot who flew me here from the big island before."

She took a bus to the little airport.

"Sorry, miss," the man in the terminal office said. "The Thursday flight to Isla Grande left half an hour ago. We won't be going again till Tuesday."

"Five days!" Alex exclaimed. "I can't wait that long!"

"Well, there's a cruise ship coming in this afternoon."

"I'll take it," said Alex.

"It's going all the way to New York City, if you like."

"I'd like," said Alex.

As the man processed her ticket, Alex looked around the terminal. In a little bookstore just across from her, she saw a sign:

COMING SOON:
THE NEWEST BOOK BY ALEX ROVER!
NO DETAILS REVEALED
UNTIL PUBLICATION DATE: JULY 14!
BUY IT HERE SOON!

"What's the name on the ticket?" the man asked.

"Al . . ." Alex looked at the sign again and shuddered. "Alice. Alice Dozer."

She signed for it quickly so he wouldn't notice that it wasn't exactly the same name as on her credit card.

Then she went to the dock to wait for the ship.

"It's simple," Nim told Fred. "All we have to do is search the ship, and we'll find Selkie."

The Kids' Klub was in the stern, so they walked past the long rows of locked cabin doors to the set of stairs and elevators in the bow.

13 Eagle
12 Flamingo
11 Sea Lion
10 Armadillo
9 Toucan
8 Chinchilla
7 Parrot
6 Monkey
5 Butte
4 Couga
3 Dolp
2 Pira
1 Anaco

"Up or down?" Nim asked Fred.

Fred couldn't decide, but the animal buttons in the elevator showed that the Armadillo Deck was the tenth one above the water and there were only three more decks above it. The next level up was the Sea Lion Deck.

Aha! Nim thought, and raced up the stairs.

They came out into bright sunshine and saw a small pool with a flat rock in the middle and a wall around the edge saying SEA LION DECK.

But there were no sea lions inside it.

Grabbing her shell whistle, Nim blew two long, shrill notes that would call Selkie in from the farthest reef at home on the island.

But Selkie didn't come. Nim looked for her in the huge swimming pool with the long, curving waterslide and in the hot bubbling pool where people lazed the way Nim liked to float in her own Rainforest Pool. The only sea lions she could find anywhere were plastic, set out on a giant chessboard with other life-sized animal pieces.

And beyond the ship, whichever way Nim looked, there was nothing but empty sea. Her island was far, far away.

"Even if we find her," she said to Fred, "how are we going to get home?"

Fred stared hard.

"You're right!" Nim said. "The important thing is to find her—we can figure out how to escape once we're all together."

The next deck up was the Flamingo, where two long-legged pink birds stood in a shallow pond inside their narrow cage. People at white tables sipped drinks while others *whoosh*ed screaming down the waterslide into the Sea Lion Deck pool. Nim thought about how much Selkie would love the slide. Fred tickled under her chin to say he'd like to try it too.

Upstairs, at the very top of the ship, there was only a half deck, where joggers in shorts ran on a track through an aviary of eagles.

"So now we have to go down," Nim said. She decided to take the elevator—and even though her stomach still flip-flopped, it wasn't quite so bad now that she knew it was going to happen.

They went down past the Flamingo and Sea Lion decks, past the Armadillo Deck, where the Kids' Klub was, and got out on the Toucan Deck. It had a path outside, where people leaned over the railing to gaze out to sea, and inside was a hall down the middle with cabins on either side.

In every deck's hall was a cage, tank, or pool with the animals the deck was named after. After the toucans were chinchillas and then parrots, but the one that made Nim feel the saddest and sickest of all was the cage with six frightened baby spider monkeys.

And on the Monkey Deck, down the outside path on each side of the ship, was a row of lifeboats, hoisted high on strong steel frames, with a cover like a little roof on top of each one. Most were big enough to hold lots of people, but in the middle was a small inflatable motorboat with a canvas cover on top, just like the one that had picked Nim up this morning. Exactly like the one that had seal-napped Selkie.

Nim blew her shell whistle again, loud and clear, under that boat and under the one on the other side of the ship.

But there was no answer, not the slightest *thump* or *whuffle*.

Nim ran on down to the Butterfly Deck, which was full of rooms with things to buy and rooms with food and drink—but most of all, full of people.

People, people, people! Nim thought. *So, so, so many!*

It was like being in the middle of sun-baking sea lions, but noisier.

She opened a door to a wonderful library full of books and quiet, but she couldn't hide there until she'd found Selkie. Behind another door, amidst a room of smiling people, a woman with a long white dress and flowers in her hair was walking up the aisle to a man who looked so happy he was nearly crying.

A wedding! Nim thought. *I'm seeing a real wedding!*

She felt like crying too, but not because she was happy.

Nim and Fred looked in cafés and restaurants, beauty salons and barbershops, dress stores and pajama stores, sports stores and toy stores. On the next deck, they watched a cougar snarling as it paced its cramped cage in a room with bright lights and red velvet. They searched in video arcades, piano bars, and theaters. They were back down on the deck where they'd come on board, but there was still no sign of Selkie.

Fred rubbed his spiky back against Nim's neck.

"You're right," she said. "We'll find her. We just have to keep going."

Down the stairs Nim ran, down to the lowest deck of all.

There weren't any people on this deck; the engine's deep *rumble* was louder and *thump*ed more strongly through her feet, with a smell that reminded her of the seaplane. And instead of a picture of an animal at the bottom of the stairs, this deck's sign said CREW ONLY! NO PASSENGERS ALLOWED!

Nim put on her Troppo Tourist jacket.

A man in gray overalls came out of a doorway. "What are you doing here?" he demanded.

"I'm . . . I'm taking him back to the Professor," Nim said, pointing to Fred on her shoulder.

"His door's behind you."

"Thanks!" said Nim, hoping he wouldn't hear her heart, which was *thump*ing as hard as her feet on the cold steel floor. She turned to the door that said FOUNDATION FOR RESEARCH ON INTELLIGENT, UNIQUE, AND INTERESTING ANIMALS. DANGER: KEEP OUT.

Nim went in.

5

THE ROOM WAS FULL of cages and sad smells. There were parrots, songbirds, lizards, spider monkeys, and a tank of tropical fish—and Selkie! She was sleeping in a cage beside an old bathtub full of dirty seawater.

Nim raced across the room, yanked open the cage door, and threw herself onto the sea lion, hugging and kissing her, rubbing her head and tickling her whiskers. Selkie *whuffled* and opened her eyes.

"It's okay, Selkie," Nim whispered. "I've come to—"

But before she could finish the sentence, a deep voice snarled, "Hey! What are you doing here?"

Nim looked up at a tall, pale man with steel blue eyes. Nim didn't recognize him, but Jack would have, and so would Alex. This was the very same man who'd been in charge of the Troppo Tourist boat that scared Nim's mother's whale to the bottom of the sea, and also the one that had dropped off Alex and her tiny boat into the terrible storm when she came to rescue Nim.

But all Nim knew was that he was the person who'd seal-napped her friend. She was as angry as Fire Mountain when it erupted.

But she also knew she'd never get Selkie out of here if she let that fire escape.

"Are you the Professor?" she asked.

He nodded. "How did you get down here?"

"I want to work with the animals," said Nim.

The Professor laughed. "Let me guess: your mom's on the crew, she smuggled you on board—and now you're bored!"

Nim nodded as if he'd guessed her secret.

"What's your mom's name?"

"Alex," said Nim. Then she felt even worse. Her mother's name had been Emily.

"And will she think it's a good idea for you to be snooping around down here?"

"She knows I like learning about animals," Nim said quickly. "And . . . and I thought you'd like to see this marine iguana."

Fred stared hard.

"That," said the Professor, "is the ugliest thing I've ever seen. Luckily, some people like ugly creatures. Find an empty cage and stick it in."

Fred tucked himself tighter around Nim's neck.

"HE'S NOT GOING IN A CAGE!" Nim said. "Animals don't belong in cages!"

The Professor's voice was like ice. "The Foundation for Research on Intelligent, Unique, and Interesting Animals helps animals from all over the world. The most intelligent, unique, or interesting will go to millionaires' homes—I mean, be relocated to appropriate environments—at the end of the cruise."

"But . . . the iguana could learn to be even more intelligent, unique, and interesting if he knew how to live with people. Plus, I found him. He's my . . . property."

The Professor shrugged. "All the animals residing on this ship are the property of the Foundation. But if you want to tame him first, I guess I can allow that."

"We've already put on a show for the Kids' Klub."

He laughed, a thin sort of laugh. "So you fancy yourself a mini-Professor, do you? Think you could take over my job of giving animal lectures to the passengers?"

"No, no, of course not! It was just a little show for the kids. But I could help you. . . .

I've even worked with sea lions before. I bet I could teach this one all sorts of tricks!"

"That sea lion," the Professor said, "is a mean, vicious beast. It tried to bite me when I rescued it. It'll be more cooperative after a few days with no food."

Nim felt as if someone had thrown a coconut hard against her stomach. She took a deep breath. *Think, think!* she told herself. *All that matters is helping Selkie!*

"Sea lion," she announced to the cage, "your name is . . . Selkie! Selkie—come out!"

"You can't do that!" the Professor bellowed as he jumped out of Selkie's way.

"Selkie," Nim began.

The Professor grabbed a long whip from the corner of the room.

Nim looked around wildly. There was nowhere to hide. "Please don't hit her!" she screamed, and leapt in front of her friend.

"We'll get out of this somehow," she whispered to Selkie. "Just do what I say, even if it seems stupid."

"Get away from her!" the Professor snarled.

Nim ignored him. "Selkie—handstand!"

Selkie raised herself on her front flippers and did her best handstand.

What next? Nim thought desperately.

Then Fred scurried across to Selkie. He rolled himself into a ball.

"Oh, Fred!" said Nim.

Fred rolled himself tighter.

"Selkie," said Nim, "soccer!"

Selkie sat thinking with her head on one side, the way she did when she was puzzling about something tricky. Nim always shouted at her when she threw Fred instead of the coconut when they played soccer, and Fred always sulked.

"Soccer!" Nim said again.

Selkie flicked Fred up with her nose and threw him neatly to Nim. He climbed tight around Nim's neck again.

"Thank you!" said Nim. "Now give me a kiss."

Selkie waddled over and whiskery-kissed Nim on the cheek.

The Professor's eyes had opened wide with surprise. He smiled as he put down his whip. "Okay, girlie; you can help."

6

JACK SAT ON SELKIE'S ROCK till his shadow stretched dark across the beach—but the little red seaplane never came back, and neither did Nim.

"Nim!" Jack called, walking back to the new hut the three of them had built together. Nim and Jack's previous home had been blown away by the terrible storm. "Nim! Dinnertime!"

The only answer was a *honk* from a sea lion. Jack couldn't tell whether it was Selkie.

"Nim!" he called again. "Nim!"

She wasn't at the hut. She wasn't at Turtle Beach or Shell Beach, the Rainforest Pool or the vegetable garden, Keyhole Cove or Sea Lion Point.

She knows Alex has gone! Jack thought. *She doesn't want to see me because I somehow drove Alex away. Poor Nim!*

He climbed up to the Emergency Cave, because he thought she might hide there if she really didn't want to see him.

There were fresh footprints on the floor, but no Nim. And that's when Jack really started to worry.

• • •

Alex had sat so long in the Sunshine Island waiting room that the sky had turned black. Suddenly the ship floated into the harbor with its lights twinkling as if it were a fairytale castle.

But Alex didn't care about fairytales. She just wanted to go to her cabin, lock the door, and not come out till she got to the other side of the world.

There were no portholes in the Animal Room, but Nim felt the engines stop and the ship bump gently against a wharf.

Now! We can escape! Nim thought, rubbing Selkie's head in a get-ready way. Fred was already tucked tight on her shoulder, worn out after his busy day.

"Okay, young one," said the Professor. "Time to get that sea lion back into its cage."

"But—"

The Professor pointed his whip at her. "Let's get things straight. Out of the goodness of my heart, I'm going to let you help me with these animals. But if you don't do exactly what I say, when I say it, I'll have to tell the captain that your mom smuggled a stowaway on board. Then he'll have to tell the police—and then you and Alex will go to jail."

Nim nodded.

She hugged Selkie, hard, then let her go. It felt like the second-worst thing she'd ever done.

Selkie slid slowly into her cage.

"Now scram. I don't want your mom snooping around here looking for you."

"She wouldn't do that!" Nim spluttered, though she wasn't sure if she was defending her real mother or Alex.

The Professor laughed, pushed her out the door, and locked it.

There was nothing Nim could do but walk back up the hall and up the stairs as if she knew where she was going.

"Fred," she whispered when they were alone, "what are we going to do?"

Fred made his hungry face, which wasn't any help at all.

Nim got into the elevator, pushed the ARMADILLO button, and went back to the Kids' Klub. No one was there. Nim and Fred curled up in a chair to share the banana in her pocket— but she'd seen two women cleaning the Troppo Tots' room next door, and Nim knew that if they came in here they'd tell her to get out and go back to her cabin. Even with Fred on her shoulder, Nim felt alone, very small, and very, very frightened. She needed to find somewhere safe to sleep.

An empty soda bottle rolled out from under a chair.

Nim thought of how she and Jack always checked bottles when they drifted in with the tide. "There might be a message," Jack always said. So far, there never had been—but they liked imagining that someday there might be.

Paper and pencils were stacked on a desk. Nim peeked out the door: the women were still washing the Troppo Tots' floor. She had maybe a minute before they found her.

Dear Jack,

The Troppo Tourists have seal-napped Selkie. Fred and I are on the ship too. We will rescue Selkie as soon as we can, but she is locked up tonight.

I'm very, very sorry I made Alex leave.

Love (as much as Selkie loves fish),

Nim

Nim walked down the stairs to the next deck, and then down to the next and the one after that, because she didn't know where to go or what else to do. She could see lights on the wharf and in the houses behind it, as if everyone had a flashlight or candles in their windows. It looked like a scene out of a fairytale.

Other people were looking out too, leaning on the railings and chatting. Some of them smiled and said hello, but Nim kept on walking, around to the other side of the ship. No one was on that side because there was nothing to look at except the black and empty sea, and nothing to do unless you were a lonely Nim throwing her message in a bottle far into the darkness, hoping the waves would float it to Jack.

She went down the next stairs to the Monkey Deck—where the lifeboats were. She stopped under the small inflatable motorboat. "Hang on, Fred," said Nim.

Swinging upside down like a nimble monkey-girl, Nim scrambled up the frame and onto the boat, unclipped one end of the canvas cover, and slid inside. Then she pulled out four life jackets to make a mattress and pillow, and curled up.

Fred went straight to sleep, but Nim kept seeing Selkie locked in her cage, and Alex flying away on the plane, and Jack all alone on their island. She didn't know how she was going to save Selkie, or where they were going to end up, or how they were going to live on this ship.

For the first time since she was a baby, Nim cried herself to sleep.

Nim was so tired, and the canvas lifeboat cover kept the sun out so well, that she didn't wake up till long after the sun was up and the ship was back out at sea.

She opened her eyes, peeked quickly over the edge of the lifeboat—and ducked down even faster, because a boy was coming out of the cabin in front of her!

Nim settled back down to wait. Fred made a hungry face, so she dug through all her pockets to see what she could find: a pencil and a very soggy notebook, a green stone, five ankle bands for birds visiting the island, a small bamboo cup, a few strands of seaweed . . . and the map Alex had drawn of her city island.

She gave Fred the seaweed and, very gently, spread Alex's map out on the seat. It was torn on the fold lines and a bit faded.

MAP: NEW YORK CITY/MANHATTAN ISLAND

"You'd probably be grounded all the way to New York City," Kylie had said when they pulled Nim out of the sea.

New York City was where Alex's editor was—the one person in the world who would know where Alex was now.

"Oh, Fred, we're going to rescue Selkie, find Alex—and bring us all together again!" she whispered. "All we have to do is stay on the ship till the end of the trip—without getting caught."

Then there was a *thump*, and a *bump*, and a boy slithered into Nim's boat.

7

Nim and the boy stared at each other.

Fred and the boy stared at each other.

"Ben!" a girl called. "What are you doing?"

Ben didn't answer.

"I'm coming up too!"

Nim's boat rocked again, and Erin slithered in.

"Be quiet!" Ben hissed. "She's a stowaway!"

"I thought you were the Professor's kid!"

"I didn't mean to stow away," Nim explained, "but the Professor kidnapped Selkie."

"Kidnapped!" Erin and Ben whispered together, crouching closer toward her in the bottom of the lifeboat.

"Who's Selkie?" asked Erin.

"She's our best friend! She's a sea lion."

"How are you going to rescue her all by yourself?" asked Ben.

So Nim told them her story. It was hard for Erin and Ben to believe, but they knew it was true.

"We'll help!" said Erin.

"It's not going to be easy," said Nim. "We need to make a plan."

"But first, we all need breakfast," said Ben. Fred lifted his head and stared. He liked this Ben.

"You exit first, Ben," said Erin. "No one's ever surprised to see you popping out of strange places."

With a quick peek over the edge, Ben swung down, and a second later he rapped twice on the metal frame to say the coast was clear. Erin followed. After a while there were two more raps, and Nim climbed out too. Erin was waiting at the open door of the cabin; Nim could see a man and a woman disappearing down the stairs with two small girls and Ben.

"Come inside, quick!" Erin whispered.

This cabin was bigger and fancier, with two beds and two sets of drawers and lamps, a desk, and a closet.

"Mom and Dad and the twins are in the cabin next door," Erin said, "but they've gone to breakfast now, so we'll be okay." She opened the closet. "I've got some clothes for you."

"But I've got clothes," said Nim.

"Your shorts are great," Erin said, "but if you're going to hide on the ship, you need to look like the other kids."

Erin was right, Nim thought.

In the bathroom, Erin gave Nim a bag with a toothbrush, a tiny tube of toothpaste, and a comb. "We got these on the plane. Meet us at the Kids' Klub after you've visited Selkie— we'll bring you some breakfast."

Erin raced out to meet up with her family, and Nim had a shower. This time she closed the shower door so Fred couldn't run in and out. She hung her towel up where Erin had shown her, changed into her new clothes, and slipped out of the cabin, her rubber thongs flip-flopping a strange music on her feet.

Down in the hold, the Animal Room was still locked. Nim sat outside the door, calling to Selkie through the crack, but she couldn't hear any *whuffles* on the other side. Finally the Professor came to unlock it, yawning and grumbling.

Selkie was sitting up in her cage, looking cross and bored. Nim rushed to her.

"Never hug the animals!" the Professor snarled.

"I only do it to help them learn tricks," said Nim.

The Professor grunted. "So what do you think you could teach them?"

"I'll bet the sea lion could catch fish," said Nim.

Selkie barked yes.

Nim threw two fish high and twirling, and Selkie caught them both.

"That's enough," snapped the Professor. "She needs to be hungry enough to learn something more interesting."

"She could probably do much better tricks in the water," said Nim.

The Professor pointed to the bathtub.

"That's not big enough!" But Selkie slid into it, because if she rolled and splashed, at least she could get wet.

The Professor sneered. "She's just too fat!"

Selkie glared and slid out of the tub—and Fred scrabbled from Nim's shoulder into the bit of water left behind, checking for seaweed.

Nim threw a fish into the tub. Fred didn't eat fish, so he flicked it over the edge to Selkie. Selkie opened her mouth, and the fish disappeared.

"If they had a pool to practice in," said Nim, "they could do fantastic tricks. Really, I'm an expert."

"Hmph," said the Professor. Nim wished she knew what that "hmph" meant, but at least he let her give Selkie the rest of her breakfast fish. She put out seeds for the birds too, and fruit for the monkeys and lizards, but most of the animals cowered at the back of their cages, too frightened to eat.

Fred clung tight to Nim's shoulder. He was too afraid of being locked up to even steal food from the other lizards.

Selkie stuck close to Nim's side, *whuffl*ing worriedly. She was afraid of being locked up again too, but she was more worried about what the bad man might do to Nim.

And so when the Professor ordered Selkie to her cage and Nim out of the room, Selkie didn't complain so that Nim wouldn't worry, and Nim didn't cry so that Selkie wouldn't worry.

Fred just waited till the Professor had gone the other way

down the hall, with the key in his pocket—then he sneezed, hard.

After the gray misery of the Animal Room, the Kids' Klub seemed like a strange kind of dream, with too many lights, too many colors, too much noise.

"Come on," said Erin, "let's go outside."

They ran up the stairs to the Sea Lion Deck. "The perfect spot for planning a sea lion rescue!" Ben exclaimed.

It was hard not to feel a little happier as they lounged in the deck chairs beside the great blue pool, looking out over the deeper blue sea. Erin gave Nim a peanut butter sandwich on fresh white bread. The peanut butter was sticky, but Nim liked it after the first few bites. Ben had a banana in his pocket that was only a little bit squashed, and a piece of watermelon in a napkin that was completely smashed.

Fred loved the smashed watermelon.

And as they ate and talked, their plan grew—and grew and grew.

Alex Rover had no plans at all. Not one.

A young woman, with VIRGINIA on her name tag, knocked on her door with a glass of "good morning" juice. "I'm your steward for the trip, Ms. Dozer—is there anything I can do to help you settle in?"

"Could you have all my meals sent to my cabin, please?"

"Sure!" said Virginia. "But I hope you're feeling well enough to get out and do things soon. The Professor's lecturing on spider monkeys this afternoon. Poor little things . . . anyway, the Professor says they don't mind being away from their mothers, and he's the expert! So maybe you'll feel well enough to go to that."

"Maybe," said Alex. Then she remembered that she'd been wearing the same blue T-shirt and red pants for two days and a night. "Is there anywhere on the ship to buy clothes?"

Virginia smiled. "Clothes, jewelry, sports gear . . . we've got absolutely everything!" She handed Alex a phone directory from the desk. "Do you know we've actually got one old lady who lives on the ship full-time? She says she never intends to go ashore again, because the ship has everything a city does and it's easier to get around. I'm sure you'll find what you need."

Alex flipped through the directory and phoned the Troppo Ladies' Leisurewear Shoppe to order a few new pairs of shorts and tops.

But when she opened her mouth, she heard herself ask for pajamas, because deep down, all she really wanted to do was stay in her bed until she had to get off the ship.

Maybe she'd become like the old lady and just stay on this ship for the rest of her life.

• • •

Jack had searched for Nim from one end of the island to the other and across the other side. When the sun came up, he was on top of Fire Mountain.

Far below him were Frigate Bird Cliffs, Turtle Beach's pale gold sand, the grasslands and Shell Beach, the hut, Sea Lion Point, Keyhole Cove, and finally the grim black lava rock where the Emergency Cave was hidden.

But no matter which way or how far his binoculars searched, there was no sign of Nim.

"She's not on the island," Jack finally admitted to himself. "And Selkie would never let her fall into the sea and drown. She must be with Alex."

The picture of the seaplane leaving was burned into his

mind, but when he tried to decide if he could have seen the top of Nim's wild hair in the back, behind Alex's gold head, sometimes he could and sometimes he just couldn't.

Jack was angry because they'd left without telling him, and he was frightened for Nim because she'd never been in a city before, even though he knew she'd be safe with Alex. But most of all Jack was sad because he was on the island without them and they were somewhere else without him, and they should all be together.

"Well, I'll simply have to go and find them," said Jack.

The problem was, he had absolutely no idea where to look.

8

TWELVE WEEKS AGO, a storm had taken Jack's boat. The same storm that had brought Alex to the island. The boat never came back—and Jack hadn't yet built a new one.

He'd have to take the seaplane, just like Alex and Nim. With a bit of luck, by the time it got here, he'd know where he was going.

Jack ran, slid, and skidded all the way down Fire Mountain back to the hut. He turned on the computer and checked his e-mails just in case there was one from Alex, and when there wasn't, he wrote one to her.

To: aka@incognito.net
From: jack.rusoe@explorer.net
Date: Friday 9 July, 7:03 a.m.
Subject: WHERE ARE YOU?
Dear Alex,
Why did you go? Where have you gone?

Why did you take Nim without telling me?

Please give her this message:

Dear Nim,
Stay with Alex; I'm coming.
Love,
Jack

Then, to make sure Nim knew he meant it, he added:

(as much as Selkie loves the ocean)

Next he wrote:

To: delia.defoe@papyrus.publishing.com
From: jack.rusoe@explorer.net
Date: Friday 9 July, 7:05 a.m.
Subject: Alex Rover
Dear Delia,
Alex has disappeared. She's taken Nim. Do you know where she's gone?
Yours truly,
Jack Rusoe

Finally he wrote:

To: seaplane@sunshineisland.com

From: jack.rusoe@explorer.net

Date: Friday 9 July, 7:08 a.m.

Subject: EMERGENCY!

Please return to the island where you brought supplies yesterday morning. I need to leave immediately.

Urgently,

Jack Rusoe

The computer dinged before he'd even had time to stand up.

To: jack.rusoe@explorer.net

From: delia.defoe@papyrus.publishing.com

Date: Friday 9 July, 7:09 a.m.

Subject: re: Alex Rover

Thank you for your e-mail. I'm presently out of the office, due to the preparations for the launch of Alex Rover's exciting new book on July 14. I can assure you, it will be worth the wait!

As you can appreciate, there is a large backlog of e-mails at this time; however, I will do my best to reply within five working days.

Regards,

Delia Defoe

"Five working days!" Jack shouted. "I can't wait that long!"

The computer dinged again.

To: jack.rusoe@explorer.net
From: seaplane@sunshineisland.com
Date: Friday 9 July, 7:10 a.m.
Subject: I'm on vacation!
I am going on vacation, so Sunshine Seaplane will be closed from Thursday evening, July 8, to Monday, August 30. I hope this doesn't cause any inconvenience.

This is an automated response. Please do not reply, as this mailbox will not be checked until August 30.

Happy traveling!

Sam
Sunshine Seaplane

"How am I going to travel?" Jack shouted. "And," he added as he typed "Troppo Tourists" into the search box, "I'M NOT HAPPY!"

Jack thought their island was the most beautiful island in the whole world, with birds and animals who were free and happy. He had tried to hide it from the Troppo Tourists, because he knew that if they came, they'd drive away the birds and animals and pick the plants—and then it wouldn't be the most beautiful island in the world anymore.

But here's the thing—Jack loved Nim more than he hated the Troppos. And since they'd brought Alex nearly all the way from Sunshine Island, maybe they could take him back.

**GOODBYE ADVENTURE CHARTERS!
HELLO LUXURY CRUISES!
BIGGER AND BETTER IN EVERY WAY!
The Troppo Tourists have said farewell to the charter ship
that took you on so many adventurous tours.
So come and join us on our glorious
new luxury cruise ship! Click here for schedules.**

Jack couldn't bear to read any more. He switched off the computer.

"Luxury cruises!" he muttered, pulling the sleeping mats away from a wall.

The wall was built of strong bamboo poles, firmly laced together. It was the only one without a window. Jack grabbed the ax from behind the hut.

"Here's to happy traveling!" he shouted, and chopped a raft-sized square out of the wall. He nailed a blanket across the hole, to keep out the dust and birds, and put an empty bag over the computer and science stuff. "That'll have to do!" declared Jack.

With a thick rope, Jack hauled his raft across the sand to Shell Beach. He was hot, tired, and thirsty when he finished, but he stopped only long enough to split a coconut and drink its milk. It was strange not to have Fred begging for the coconut meat.

Fred might be on a plane! Jack thought, and he almost smiled as he raced up the hill to Tabletop Garden.

Jack found two strong, slim lengths of bamboo just the right size for a mast and a crossbar, chopped them down, and raced back to the beach. He lashed the crossbar to the mast, cut a neat hole out of the center of his raft, and then, with wires and rope and bits of bamboo, fixed the mast in place.

"At least the sail will be easy," said Jack. He pulled out a bag he'd unloaded from the seaplane just the day before, containing a sail for the boat he'd planned to build. It was a perfect, clean white sail, light and strong enough to catch any wind— but it was too tall and too wide for his little makeshift raft.

Jack had never had a brand-new sail before.

He took out his fat red pocketknife, cut a big square from the sail, and rigged it to the mast.

Then he stuffed six coconuts, a change of pants and shirt, and his toothbrush into the sail bag, dropped his compass into one of his pockets and his notebook and pen in another, and grabbed two fishing lines, two big containers of water, and some bananas.

Finally, he opened a metal box. It hadn't been opened for a long, long time, but his wallet, checkbook, and passport were still there, clean and dry. Jack dropped them into his extra-safe pocket—the one with a loop and a string to tie it shut—and walked out of the hut.

● ● ●

"Do you know Alex Rover?" Nim asked Erin. She'd waited till Ben had gone to get ice cream, because some things are easier to tell one person than two.

"The famous writer?"

"She's my friend," said Nim. "And my dad's friend. But I was mean to her, and now she's gone home."

"Everybody's mean sometimes," said Erin, though Nim knew Erin could never be as mean as she had been.

"My dad will be worrying that she'll never come back," said Nim, "and he might be worried about me too. Or . . . he might be glad I'm gone."

"He won't be glad you're gone," said Erin.

"I wish I could tell him where I am," said Nim.

"You could e-mail him from the computer room."

"Parents have to log their kids in," said Ben, handing them each an ice cream cone.

"Write down the message and the address," said Erin, "and I'll send it."

"Thanks," said Nim. "Whew! I never knew ice cream was so *cold*!"

To: jack.rusoe@explorer.net
From: erin@kidmail.com
Date: Friday 9 July, 11:05 a.m.
Subject: Don't worry!

Dear Jack,

My friend Erin is sending this because I can't go to the computer room unless you sign me in.

I hope you got my message in a bottle. I'm on the Troppo Tourist ship heading toward New York City.

We have a plan but I don't want to write it down in case someone sees the note when Erin is writing it.

I cleaned out the birdcages this morning, and four flaming orange doves had our island's bands on their legs. I didn't know people were allowed to catch animals just because they're intelligent, unique, or interesting. The Professor says that's the best way to keep them safe. I didn't know that either. It's strange because I don't think he really likes animals.

I'm very, very sorry I was mean to Alex, and I know I was mean to you sometimes when you were talking to Alex. I wish I hadn't been.
Love (as much as Fred loves Selkie),
Nim

She wrote one to Alex too, but in the end she couldn't

bear for Erin to read it, so she crumpled it up and put it in her pocket.

"It's Pizza Night in the Kids' Klub," Ben announced, "so we can all have dinner there."

"What's pizza like?" asked Nim.

Ben explained. "But you can't ask anyone except us stuff like that! They'll guess . . ."

"That I'm a stowaway?"

"Or they might just think you're weird," said Ben, "and that'll make them notice you. Even more than Fred."

So when Erin came back from e-mailing, they found a spot behind a big white chest labeled LIFE JACKETS, up near the bow, where it was too windy for most people to sit, and Nim got lessons on how to look as if she belonged to parents on a cruise ship.

It was sort of like schoolwork with Jack, except that instead of learning about what turtles ate and how plankton grew, she was learning about what kids ate and what they said, what they did and what they had.

"There's so much stuff!" Nim groaned. "And so much to learn! How am I going to remember it all?"

"Stick with us," said Erin. "Just do what we do."

As Ben looked at his watch, Nim looked up at the sun. "But first," she said, "Fred and I have to visit Selkie."

9

SELKIE AND FRED both knew lots of tricks—but they did them only when *they* wanted to. It was hard for Nim to make them understand that to outsmart the Professor, they had to do the tricks Nim wanted when she asked.

And the Professor was watching. He was in a very bad mood because one of the baby spider monkeys had bitten him while he was giving his lecture.

First Nim fed the birds, chirping quietly to them.

"If you make bird noises, they'll never learn to talk!" the Professor snapped. "Teach them 'Pretty Polly'! That's what people pay for . . . are interested in." He stomped out the door.

Nim clucked to the doves once more and rushed to open Selkie's cage. Selkie *whuffled* and sniffed her all over, as if Nim were the one who'd been seal-napped and locked up.

"We'll get home somehow," Nim promised. "Because even if Alex doesn't like me anymore, I know she'll help us.

"The important thing is to escape. We've got five days to get ready."

She looked at Selkie's little cage and the cloudy tub of water. Five days seemed like forever.

"If I could just get you into a pool . . . ," she said.

Very quietly, she turned the door handle. It wasn't locked. She opened it a crack and peered down the hall.

The Professor was coming back!

Nim shut the door quickly and hugged Selkie hard. Just for a minute she thought she was going to cry—but that would upset Selkie.

And it was crying that got us into this mess in the first place! Nim thought, which suddenly seemed so silly she almost laughed—except now the Professor was in the room again, so instead she clapped.

"Fantastic!" she said, as if Selkie had just done the most wonderful trick in the world.

Then she added quickly, "That's enough training for today."

The Professor grunted. "Okay, kid. Get the rest of those animals fed and their cages cleaned out. If you do a good job, I'll let you do some more training in the morning."

"Thank you," Nim said politely. She worked as slowly and carefully as she could, because every minute she was here was a minute Selkie wasn't locked in her cage all alone.

Suddenly she spotted a key hanging behind the door. It looked just like the Professor's, but she'd seen him drop his into his pocket. This one had to be a spare—and if it was a spare, he might not notice if it was missing!

So Nim brushed the rotten fruit and droppings out of the monkeys' cage, put in clean water and not-quite-rotten fruit, and murmured quietly to them, trying not to let them feel how mad and sad she was to see them there. Finally she put Selkie back in her cage, sitting beside her for a long moment to rub her head with love and cool water.

"Just remember," the Professor said with his sneering smile, "the animals down here are our little secret. The Foundation's work is very important—much too important for most people to understand. I don't ever want to hear you talking about the animals down here.

"So, my little stowaway friend, just keep your mouth shut and everyone will be happy: I'll get what I've earned, the animals will get lovely new homes where people appreciate how intelligent, unique, and interesting they are—and you and your mom will stay out of jail."

Nim swallowed hard and nodded. He wanted her to be afraid, and she was. More afraid than she'd ever been. She was so afraid, the Professor knew he didn't have to worry about her at all. He sat calmly down in his chair in the corner, opened a can of soda, and started to read his newspaper.

"I'll come back in the morning," Nim whispered.

The Professor grunted and turned a page.

Nim backed to the door—and, as she waved goodbye to Selkie, snatched the key off its hook.

THE HARDEST THING about fitting in at Pizza Night, Nim decided, was acting as if the biggest thrill in her life were getting a slice with pepperoni, especially when she really wanted anchovies (anchovies were fish and tasted a bit like home).

"It's like swimming with a new pod of dolphins," she told Ben and Erin when they took their pizzas out to the deck.

"I wish I could do that!" Ben exclaimed.

"I wish we could go to your island," Erin said.

"I wish you could too," said Nim. Saying it made her feel hot inside, as if she were betraying Jack—but it was true. She used to wonder what it would be like to have friends who could talk. Now that she'd found out, she liked it. Nim wanted to be back on her island more than anything else, but she didn't want to lose Erin and Ben.

She told them what the Professor had said.

"Jail!" repeated Erin.

"But *he's* the bad guy!" Ben said fiercely.

"He says he's allowed to catch the animals because of this Foundation. He says that's the law, because catching them educates people and protects other animals all around the world."

"And he *is* a Professor," said Erin.

"And I *am* a stowaway," said Nim.

"But he's still bad," said Ben.

"We should ask Mom and Dad," said Erin.

"No!" shouted Nim. "He said he'd send me to the captain if I ever told anyone. I shouldn't even have told you—and if you help me, you'll get into trouble too!"

"We don't care if we get in trouble," Ben said.

"All that matters," Erin agreed, "is keeping you safe and getting Selkie free. So we just have to stick to our plan."

"But the best thing we can do right now," said Ben, "is try to look like we're having a good time. Let's get some more pizza!"

Fred rubbed his spiny back against Ben's leg. Fred had mozzarella strings tangled from his grinning mouth to his claws. He liked pizza, and he liked Ben more and more and more.

Nim felt lonely, climbing back up into her lifeboat with Fred while Erin and Ben stood watch outside their cabin door.

And when she pulled the cover over, it felt dark—black as the deepest sea.

Then she heard a knock—the three quick knocks and two

slow that were their signal—and felt the rocking of someone climbing the metal struts. Ben stuck his head in to hand her a flashlight.

Nim turned it on and saw why Erin had looked as if she were going to burst with her own secret when she'd said, "Sleep tight, Nim!"

The boat had been turned into a bedroom. There were two blankets to sleep on, two towels for covers, a pillow for her and one for Fred, a bottle of water, and a banana.

But best of all was remembering the look on Erin's and Ben's faces when she'd shown them the key she'd snatched. They'd touched it as if it were magic—and even though Nim wasn't a magician, just knowing it was in her pocket made her feel powerful.

It was so early the sun wasn't up when Erin rapped three "wake up!" knocks on the strut.

Still half asleep, Nim dropped her pillows and blankets over the side, just in case a Troppo Tourist used the boat during the day. Then she swung down to the deck, with Fred following. The cool morning air woke them quickly. While Erin tiptoed back into her cabin to hide the bedding, Nim and Fred raced down to the Animal Room. When there was no one around to step on him, Fred liked walking.

After a quick check to make sure no one was watching,

Nim unlocked the door and they slipped inside.

"Hurry!" she whispered to Selkie as she undid the cage. She felt sorry for the others, but she couldn't help them yet.

Selkie lolloped down the hall after her and into the elevator, *honk*ing with surprise when it went up. Fred grinned a little wider, as if he'd been doing this since he was hatched.

It was dark and deserted as they came out onto the Sea Lion Deck. They raced to the waterslide pool and dived into the clear water.

Selkie snorted and rolled, dived and leapt, around and around the pool as if she were training for the race of her life. Fred sank to the bottom and came up again, sneezing with disgust because he couldn't find any seaweed.

Nim swam with Selkie and dived with Fred; she couldn't swim as fast as a sea lion or hold her breath as long as a marine iguana, but it felt good to try. She didn't know exactly how they were going to escape, but she did know they'd all need to be as strong, as fast, and as good at everything as they could possibly be.

The sky began to pale. A man hurried past, buttoning his white chef's jacket.

Nim signaled to Selkie, and Selkie dived as silently as a whisper. Fred was already down at the bottom again; he was sure there must be seaweed somewhere. Nim kept on swimming and tried not to splash.

"You're up early!" the chef called. "Trying to beat the rush?"

"Yes," said Nim, and he hurried on by.

Nim knew it would be too dangerous to stay any longer. They slipped out and went back to the hold, with nothing but a quickly drying trail of water to tell where they'd been.

11

JACK WOKE UP WITH the sun. He'd steered all night, with a few quick naps in between. Daylight showed him that he still had a long, long way to go—there was no sign of land in all this wide blue sea.

A frigate bird circled low to see if he had any fish. "Nothing today, Galileo!" Jack called. He wished he could tuck a note into the big bird's leg band, but even Galileo couldn't find Nim in a city.

For just a minute Jack wondered what he'd do if Nim wasn't with Alex—but he pushed that thought away.

As Galileo disappeared into the sky, Jack called out, "You're right, I should put those lines out now! Thanks for reminding me!"

He checked his compass, adjusted the sail to head four points farther east, threw his fishing lines in, and had a drink of water and some coconut for breakfast.

"I'll be with you soon, Nim!" he called.

Then he added more quietly, "And you too, Alex. I hope."

• • •

Alex woke with a start. She was sure someone had knocked on her cabin door: three quick raps. Then there was a *thump* of someone jumping onto the deck, and whispering.

It was just the children from the cabin next door. She'd heard them during the day; it sounded as if there were two very little girls, a boy and another girl about Nim's age, and maybe even another girl. She could never hear what they said, just the buzz of their voices and *thumps* from their cabin when they jumped to the floor.

Alex wondered what they were like. *Maybe they'd know how to be friends with Nim,* she thought. *Maybe I'd have been better at it if I'd met other kids before I went to the island. . . .*

"If you'd been better at it," she told herself, "you wouldn't be on this ship right now!"

"And don't you dare cry again!" she added, and made herself go back to sleep.

Nim had got Selkie back just in time. It was now bright, busy daylight, and people were swarming everywhere, settling into deck chairs and crowding the rails. Someone would have probably noticed a sea lion galumphing through the ship.

It was busy out on the water too. There were more ships ahead, behind, and coming toward them. They were going down a wide river with bright green hills close on either side, and Nim felt tight and closed in when she could see only a narrow strip of water instead of the wide blue sea she was used to.

The river became skinnier and the banks grew steeper, until it was such a narrow canal their ship was nearly touching both concrete sides. Very gently, they were tugged up to a pair of giant locked doors. Another pair of doors shut behind them—and just as Nim was wondering where the ship could go next, it started going up as if it were in an elevator!

Nim tried to look as if she were used to being on ships that went up and down elevators, until she saw that nearly everyone on board had come out to gawk and take pictures.

"Amazing!"

"How does it work?"

"The water comes in through culverts from a lake."

"I've wanted to see this all my life!"

But everything's strange to me! thought Nim. *How am I supposed to know which things are strange to everyone else?*

She saw Erin and Ben, with their parents and little sisters, watching from outside their cabin while their mother videotaped the giant elevator doors.

Now the dock on the other side of the railing was the same height as the deck. If she jumped over the railing right now, she could probably escape the ship.

"But we can't leave without Selkie," she whispered to

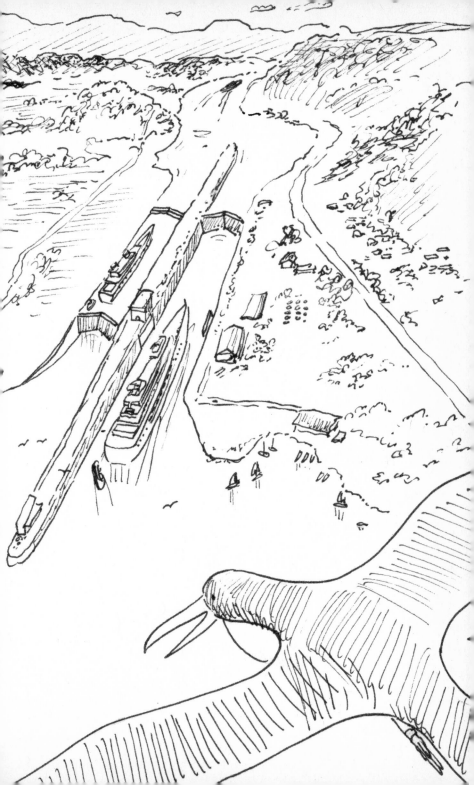

Fred. Fred rubbed his head under her chin.

The ship went up higher and higher till they were way too far above the dock to jump.

Anyway, thought Nim, *if we got off here, how will I ever find Alex?*

And how will I ever find home?

That afternoon in the Kids' Klub, Kelvin taught them to play Spiderweb. The person who was the Spider stood in the middle with hands above their head. Then all the other kids squashed up around them. When Kelvin shouted "Web!" each kid had to reach behind and grab the first two hands they met, and keep holding on to them while everyone wiggled around, forward and backward, to make a circle—while the Spider tried to break through.

Nim was good at being the Spider, because she could squirm under arms or slither through legs faster than anyone. But what she liked best was holding tight to Erin or Ben or kids she didn't know and just being part of the web.

To: jack.rusoe@explorer.net
From: erin@kidmail.com
Date: Saturday 10 July, 5:45 p.m.
Subject: more information
Dear Jack,
I thought you might have answered by now, but I guess

you are very busy since I'm not there to help you with the science stuff.

Today the Professor took pictures of me holding the birds and caged animals. He says the Foundation likes to see pictures like this to show how intelligent, unique, and interesting the animals are, to prove that they should be protected. He dressed one of the spider monkeys up like a baby and I thought it looked so sad. I played a swinging game with it afterward to cheer it up.

Selkie is a lot happier today because she had a swim in the pool, and Fred is happy because he tasted pizza last night and today Ben also brought him a whole pocketful of salad for lunch and I've had lots of different food too. Ben and Erin said I shouldn't ask for a seaweed sandwich because people will think that's strange and they might guess I'm a stowaway. I like some of the new foods, and when you want food here you don't have to make it or catch it yourself.

I saw a frigate bird today. I wished it were Galileo with a message from you.

Love (as much as Galileo loves stealing fish),
Nim

12

"I'VE GOT AN IDEA," Nim said. It was the morning after the ship went through the elevator canal and the Professor was whistling cheerfully. Nim needed him to be in a good mood so she could start putting their plan into action. "You know how you give a lecture about animals every day? When you do the sea lion lecture on Wednesday, it could be like a show—like a circus! And I could help."

"There's not enough time to get that together."

"But this sea lion is amazingly smart—and so is the iguana. I bet I could get them ready for you, especially if I could train them in a pool."

"That beast will go to the Sea Lion Pool," snarled the Professor, "when I'm sure she won't bite anyone else."

I wish she'd bitten you harder! Nim thought.

"She was probably just scared," she said. "I'm positive she won't do it again."

"She'd better not," said the Professor, glancing at his whip.

"Everyone will see how intelligent, unique, and interesting they both are. And you'll get all the credit!"

"Well, maybe we *can* do a show on Wednesday morning. Then if she behaves, she can stay in the Sea Lion Pool till she's sol—till she's relocated."

Nim felt as if she'd just swallowed a bucket of cold water. *Relocated! How would I ever get her back then?*

But we won't let that happen! she reminded herself fiercely. *We've still got three days to get our show ready—and then we'll escape.*

"You can have a couple of hours in the afternoons to practice. And"—the Professor paused and stared at her as if he knew exactly what she was thinking—"it had better be good."

"But how's it going to be good if we can't use the big pool?" Nim demanded when she and Erin and Ben were in the Kids' Klub carving watermelons into interesting sculptures. Kristie had demonstrated how to carve a Viking's head and a sailboat, and now the kids each had a watermelon and a blunt knife and could carve whatever they liked.

Nim used her own pocketknife to carve Selkie. Erin carved a cat, and Ben made a Viking's head that was nearly as good as Kristie's.

Fred ate the whole middle out of a watermelon and made an empty rowboat. Everyone clapped, and he scrambled back onto Nim's shoulder, looking smug at how clever he was.

"Do you think that could be a trick?" Nim asked.

"I don't think so," said Erin. "But I *have* figured out how you can use the waterslide pool for your show."

This was the third day Jack had spent on his raft. He still had two coconuts and half a container of water. He was a bit sore, very stiff, and very, very tired.

But there was a line on the horizon that could have been cloud or . . . *Sunshine Island*? Jack hoped so.

The closer he sailed, the clearer and less cloudlike the line became. By noon he was sure. It was definitely land. Jack tightened the sail and whistled for wind.

A speck of light caught his eye. A soda bottle was bobbing on the waves—with something inside it.

If Nim had been with him, they would have chased and grabbed it.

But they'd never, ever found a message—and if Nim had been with him, he wouldn't be going to Sunshine Island on a raft made out of the wall of their hut. Jack let the bottle float by and sailed on as fast as he could.

Alex had spent three whole days alone in her cabin. She hadn't spoken to anyone except Virginia, the steward, when she brought her juice every morning and came back a little later to clean. "What a shame you're not feeling better!" Virginia said. "You'd have so much fun if you could get out there and meet people." But Alex had left behind the people she most wanted to know.

She even kept her curtains closed, because all she could see were people walking by and the lifeboat stands, which weren't very interesting.

And even though there were pens and writing paper in her cabin's desk, she hadn't written a word. For the first time in her life, there was no story in her head.

Worst of all, she didn't care.

To: jack.rusoe@explorer.net

From: erin@kidmail.com

Date: Sunday 11 July, 5:30 p.m.

Subject: Important!

Dear Jack,

Erin, Ben, and I have a plan. I hope it will work. Selkie
and Fred and I are going to put on a show, so we
practiced for two hours this afternoon. It's horrible
being with Selkie when the Professor's watching
because I have to pretend I don't know her, and pretend
I'm training her to do tricks, even though it's just the
games we play at home. But Selkie thinks it's better
than being in the cage, so she doesn't mind pretending.
Fred hates the Professor so much he just glares at him
all the time, but the Professor never notices.

It's very interesting being on the ship—but I still like our
island best. I hope you will stop being mad at me soon.

Love (as much as you love the island),
Nim

"No message yet," Erin said to Nim when she came back
from sending Nim's e-mail to Jack. She tried to sound as if it

wasn't important, as if she didn't know that Nim was worrying about whether Jack was too angry to answer or there was another reason that was even worse.

"Maybe he keeps forgetting to charge the battery," Nim said.

"Probably," said Erin.

"Or a virus!" said Ben.

"Maybe," said Nim.

"We've got an hour before dinner," said Ben. "Let's play Spy."

"Dolphin Deck?" asked Erin.

"Butterfly," said Nim, and started up the stairs. Ben and Erin always gave her a head start when they played Spy, because it was harder for someone with an iguana on their shoulder to blend into a crowd.

Nim chose the Butterfly Deck because the butterflies were the only animals on the ship that didn't make her feel sad. They had plenty of space to fly around, and she loved it when they landed on her hair and arms. Nim wandered slowly through the butterfly cage, with Fred sitting so still that her head and Fred's spine were soon covered with brightly colored butterflies. They both smiled so much that even the happy, kissy people who came in from the wedding room to have their pictures taken didn't notice that she didn't really belong in their party.

13

FROM ONE END of Sunshine Island to the other, people stared as Jack sailed his raft past the roaring Jet Skis, through the swimmers and snorkelers in the calm water, and right up onto the beach between the sunbathers and sandcastles.

He pulled down the sail and folded it into its bag, in case he needed it again. Curious people gathered around to watch him.

"Where's the airport, please?" Jack asked.

Someone pointed down the road.

Someone else took his picture.

"It's a long walk," one man said. "I'll drive you."

"Thanks."

Jack followed him to a golf buggy parked at the top of the beach, and the crowd drifted back to their sunbathing and sandcastles.

But when they reached the airport: "You're in luck!" said the man at the ticket counter. "You can get on a flight tomorrow morning."

"But I need to go today!" said Jack.

"Tuesdays and Thursdays—that's it."

Thursday! thought Jack. *That's the day Alex and Nim left. If they missed the flight, they'll still be here.*

The man with the golf buggy drove him all around the town till late at night, but they never found a sign of Alex or Nim.

"You," said Alex to herself as she sat cross-legged on her bunk to eat her dinner, "are a lazy, lay-a-bed, slobby slug. You've gone through the Panama Canal without even seeing it. What if you need a story hero to stow away on an oceanic adventure—how are you going to write about it?"

"Same way I always do," she answered. "Reading, research, and imagination."

"Except the last book," said Alex. "You lived that one. That's why it's your best story—and the best part of your life."

But she hadn't even been brave enough to open her new book yet.

The Kids' Klub closed at five o'clock, but a big bunch of kids were out on the Sea Lion Deck when Erin, Nim, and Ben wandered up there after dinner. Nim had just finished eating her smuggled food when a small pigtailed girl tapped Ben on the shoulder. "Spider!" she shouted.

Quick as a wink, everyone else grabbed the nearest hands to make the web; Ben wriggled and squirmed to get through and the others held tight until the pigtailed girl began to giggle and they all collapsed together in a wiggling, giggling heap, happy as a pile of sea lion pups in the sun.

Later that night, with her windows open to catch the sea breeze, Alex heard the next-door parents chatting on the deck after their children had gone to bed. She imagined them leaning over the rail to watch the moonlight dancing on the waves.

"They seem to be having a good time," the father was saying. "They've made lots of new friends."

"And they're certainly enjoying the food! They keep heaping their plates with more than they could possibly eat—but when I look again, it's gone."

"This fresh sea air's certainly giving them an appetite," the father agreed.

14

THE NEXT MORNING, Nim, Selkie, and Fred snuck out even earlier to swim in the waterslide pool. With the three of them all together, they felt almost free.

But at the first sounds of the crew bustling around, they scurried back to Selkie's prison. A few moments later, the ship dropped anchor in a white-sand harbor.

Nim locked Selkie in and ran upstairs to say good morning to the dolphins in the fountain. When she went back to the Animal Room, the Professor was waiting for her to start feeding and cleaning.

"No time for that!" he snapped as Nim hugged Selkie. "Feed them and get out. I don't want you around today."

"But you said I could practice this afternoon!"

"I've changed my mind. Now snap to it and then scram!"

His eyes were narrow, his face was hard—and he kept glancing at his whip. Nim fed the animals and got out.

"Everyone's going ashore," Erin told Nim. "I wish you could come—but they check the tickets extra carefully when people get back on. It wouldn't be safe."

"They'll probably use your inflatable," Ben added. "Did you get all your things?"

Nim nodded. Everything was tucked safely into Erin's cabin closet.

"The Kids' Klub is shut too," Erin said sadly, "so you'd better stay in our cabin."

Nim had to wander up and down the deck while Erin and Ben's mother hurried in and out of the cabins to organize their day. She felt as empty as a pricked balloon when Ben and Erin finally disappeared down the stairs with their family.

A second later, Erin came running back down the hall.

"I said I forgot my hat," she puffed, unlocking the cabin door. "There are some books on my bed, if you want to read, and television, and paper and markers for making the posters. I *wish* you could come!"

Erin grabbed her hat, then shouted, "Bye!" and ran out. Nim started looking through the books. One was *Mountain Madness* by Alex Rover. When Nim had first read it, she was alone on the island; and when Alex e-mailed to ask Jack about coconuts, Nim had answered for him. And that's how their friendship got started. Alex had tried to explain that she wasn't really the hero of her stories, but Nim hadn't believed her. She wondered if she would still like the book now that she knew Alex was just a small, scared woman—but one who'd sailed across the world to help her.

She lay on Erin's bed and started reading.

There was a knock, and Ben bounced in. "We forgot to tell you—breakfast is in the desk!"

He raced out again, and Nim found a brown-bread sandwich and an apple in the drawer.

Fred didn't like brown bread, and he didn't like apples, but he was hungry enough to share. "We'll find you something," Nim said, though she wasn't sure what.

They had a shower. Nim changed into the clothes Erin had left for her and washed hers in the sink, then sat down at the desk with the paper and colored markers. She drew twenty-two SEA LION CIRCUS posters—two for each passenger deck—exactly how she'd planned them with Erin and Ben. When she'd finished, she tucked them neatly into the desk drawer, flopped back onto Erin's bed, and went on reading.

Rap! Tap!

Someone was knocking at the door.

Nim stayed very still and didn't answer. Fred crept behind a lamp and went to sleep.

The door opened, and a steward in a white uniform and blue apron came in with a vacuum cleaner and a mop and bucket. She saw Nim and dropped her bucket.

"Yipes!" Virginia squeaked. "Did your parents leave you here alone?"

Nim nodded, because she couldn't tell the truth.

"Are you sick?"

Nim nodded again.

Virginia shook her head sympathetically. "Sorry—I still have to clean," she said, "but I'll be as quiet as I can."

She straightened Ben's bed and made Nim sit on it while she worked on Erin's. "Leaving a sick child alone!" Nim heard her muttering. "Appalling!"

Nim thought about Erin and Ben's parents, and her face grew as hot and red as the lava in Fire Mountain. "I'm feeling a lot better now!" she said.

Virginia finished cleaning, felt Nim's forehead, and made her go back to bed.

Nim picked up *Mountain Madness* again. She read lying down, she read sitting up, and she read lying on the floor with her feet on the bed. Then she practiced doing handstands, and Fred practiced climbing from her shoulder to her feet instead of the usual way around. They even made up a trick with Fred staying stiff as a log and Nim twirling him around on her feet.

But you can't stay upside down spinning an iguana forever, so after that Nim stared out through the lifeboat stands at a bit of blue sea. A great black frigate bird soared past. Looking through her spyglass, she was almost sure it was Galileo. "I wish I could go out on deck to check," she muttered, even though she didn't have a fish to call him with.

One more chapter of *Mountain Madness*; the hero had
just caught a trout in a mountain stream and cooked it over
a fire.

"I should have saved the apple for lunch," Nim told Fred.
Fred answered with his best unblinking stare. He was sure she
could find them some food if she tried hard enough.

"We can't go out," she told him, "because everyone else
has gone ashore, and the crew will notice me and ask where
my parents are."

There was another knock at the door. Nim shoved a pillow over Fred, and Virginia tiptoed in carrying a tray.

"I wasn't sure what you liked," she said, "so I brought sandwiches and salad, fruit, cake. . . ."

The pillow wiggled. Nim put her elbow on it. "Thank you. That's very nice of you."

She was glad she could say something that wasn't a lie.

"I'm so pleased you're starting to feel better. The poor lady next door hasn't left her cabin for the whole trip!"

Erin and Ben's cabin was a bright room with cheerful paintings on the walls, but Nim thought she'd have gone crazy if she'd spent the whole trip in it.

"You look a bit bored," Virginia said. "Do you want the TV on?" She handed Nim the remote control.

"Thanks," said Nim, and Virginia left to continue her cleaning.

Even though she'd seen televisions in the lounges when they'd played Spy and she'd played video games in the Kids' Klub, Nim had never sat and watched a program with a story—and she'd never used a remote. Neither had Fred. Fred didn't care about the programs, but he liked stepping on the buttons so that the channel changed just as Nim figured out what was happening.

"Cut it out, Fred!" Nim said.

Fred went to sulk under the bed, and Nim turned the TV off. She didn't want to shout again and wake up that poor sick lady next door.

"Come on . . . you can have all the lettuce," she coaxed, and when Fred had eaten the lettuce out of the sandwich and sneezed a kiwi fruit all over the bed, he felt quite cheerful again.

Nim finished *Mountain Madness* and stared out the window some more.

When she heard the *rumble* of the launches and the *thump* of passengers' feet on the gangplank, she grabbed Fred and raced outside to gulp deep breaths of fresh air.

As soon as the ship was on its way out to sea again, Nim pulled on her Troppo Tourist jacket and ran down the stairs to the Animal Room. She knocked and waited outside the door until the Professor let her in.

Selkie *whuffled* sadly, because it had been an even longer day for her. And scarier.

The last of the empty cages was full now—with long, fat snakes.

Nim found it hard writing to Jack when she couldn't say what she wanted in case someone else saw it, and when she didn't know if he was reading the e-mails or not. But she had to go on trying.

To: jack.rusoe@explorer.net
From: erin@kidmail.com

Date: Monday 12 July, 7:30 p.m.

Subject: Very important!

Dear Jack,

Maybe there's something wrong with the computer and that's why you're not answering, but I think you want to know what we're doing, so I'll go on e-mailing and maybe you can read it later.

Today I had to stay inside the cabin all day and it was very boring, but now I understand even better how Selkie must be feeling, and all the other animals with her. So maybe it was good in some ways.

Erin bought me a bead bracelet when she went ashore. It's very pretty and she bought one for herself that's just the same, so whenever we wear them we will think about each other. Ben brought Fred and me a coconut, which was good because we haven't had coconut for way too long.

Love (as much as Fred loves coconut),
Nim

15

JACK SPENT THE NIGHT on the floor of his new friend's living room.

"Who are you?" the man joked, watching Jack stare at the television as if he didn't quite know what it was. "Robinson Crusoe?"

"No—Jack Rusoe."

His friend laughed, but Jack couldn't. He'd just checked his e-mails—and not one message had come into the in-box. Only the Trash folder had blinked as the spam trickled in to be deleted.

The next morning he sorted out how to get money at the bank, and took the little plane to the airport on Isla Grande.

The only thing he could do was to go and see Alex's editor. If he met Delia Defoe and explained about Nim, she'd tell him where they were.

Jack booked the last seat left on the plane leaving the next day for New York City.

"There's a sea lion circus tomorrow," Virginia told Alex when she brought in her breakfast. "There are posters all over the ship—doesn't that sound fun?"

If Alex hadn't known Selkie, she might have thought it sounded fun. But she did know Selkie, and suddenly she missed her so much that she knew she could never see another sea lion again without crying. It was the best reason so far for staying in her cabin another day.

Erin woke Nim and Fred up earlier than usual, but they spent so long in the pool that the sun had come up before they knew it. When Nim came up for air after practicing swimming underwater, a white-uniformed crewman was standing at the edge watching.

"There's a sea lion in there!" he exclaimed.

"It's the Sea Lion Deck," said Nim.

"But this is a swimming pool. For people."

"We need it to practice for the sea lion circus," said Nim. "We won't need it after tomorrow."

"The cruise ends tomorrow!"

"That's why we won't need it," said Nim.

The crewman stared a little longer, then shrugged and walked away.

Nim and her friends scrambled out of the pool and back to the Animal Room, as fast as they could.

"I suppose you think you're clever!" the Professor snarled when he let Nim in to feed the animals. "All those posters advertising a sea lion circus at the waterslide pool—now you think I'll have to let that beast in there!"

"I must have got mixed up!" said Nim, even though the posters were exactly how she wanted them. "Isn't that what you meant?"

"I said you could have her perform a few tricks at my lecture. You know perfectly well it was supposed to be in the theater, like all my lectures. I'm a professor—that's what people expect."

"I just thought . . ."

"Just think about what's going to happen to you and your mother if you try to be too smart! Besides, no one's going to want to look at any humdrum animal tricks once we get into the harbor. You'd better do something spectacular or you won't have an audience."

"I've got something special planned," said Nim. "It'll be spectacular."

"The posters worked!" Nim said. Erin handed her a breakfast scrambled-egg sandwich and Ben tossed grapes for Fred to catch. "We can do the show the way we planned."

"And today . . ."

"We can do whatever we like."

It was hard to choose, because even though in some ways today was exactly like every other day on the ship, it was the last day they were going to spend together, and that made it special—and sad, and a little bit scary.

Fred chose to spend the day at the splash pool, where he could sit on the water jets and be blasted into the air and then paddle across the pool, just as he liked to do where the spray came in at a blowhole at the island's Black Rocks.

Ben, Erin, and Nim went on a treasure hunt with the other kids from the Kids' Klub. The clues took them all over the ship, but when Nim got to the Toucan Deck she found the toucan sitting on the floor of its cage. Its eyes were glazed and it still hadn't touched the food it had been given that morning.

Nim squatted down to see it. *It's so unhappy, it might die!* she thought. Suddenly she knew that escaping with Selkie was not enough. Every animal on the ship *had* to be rescued.

"Just hang in there a bit longer! We're going to help you all, somehow," Nim told the unhappy bird, chirping and clucking until it lifted its head to see her. When it finally began to peck its mushed mango, Nim stood up—and noticed the treasure chest hidden behind the display. It was full of enough bags of candy for everyone in the Kids' Klub.

Fred thought he liked candy, but he felt sick afterward and had to lie on his back while Nim rubbed his tummy.

Then Nim and Erin painted all the papier-mâché fish they'd been making, and Ben finished his sculpture.

"Excellent sculpture!" said the art instructor.

"It *is* pretty good," Erin admitted.

"It's amazing," said Nim.

But Fred hated it, because it looked exactly like him. He walked all around it, glaring, and then climbed up to Nim's shoulder to glare some more.

"It's so I'll remember you when you're not around," Ben explained.

Fred blinked, but Nim thought she might cry.

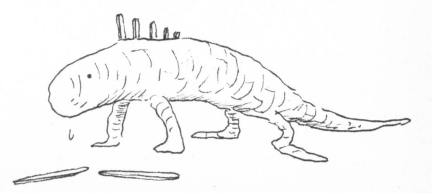

Later in the afternoon, down in the hold, Selkie and Nim
practiced handstands, and Fred practiced spinning on Selkie's
flippers. It wasn't the most important trick, but it was the start
of something bigger.

"Sleep tight," Nim whispered to Selkie when it was time
to leave. "Everything happens tomorrow."

To: jack.rusoe@explorer.net
From: erin@kidmail.com
Date: Tuesday 13 July, 5:30 p.m.
Subject: You must read this!
Dear Jack,

I haven't had an e-mail from Alex yet either, so if she is still mad at me too, this might be the last e-mail I can write to you. I don't know what I'm going to do, but I can't worry about it because first we have to get off the ship. Sometimes I wish you could sail up to the ship and rescue us, but you don't have a boat anymore, so I know you couldn't do that even if you weren't angry at me.

The Professor made me cut the bands off the island doves' legs today. But I've made notes in my notebook about the birds' markings so we can identify them again. I've made notes about all the animals on the ship because I thought you would want me to do that.

A frigate bird has been following the ship for the last three days. It's been flying too high for me to be sure but I think it really is Galileo.

I hope I'll see you and our island again very soon.

Love (as much as Selkie loves diving),
Nim

There was a special Kids' Klub dinner for the last night of the cruise, so for the first time, Nim ate in the dining room with her friends. She borrowed a skirt and top from Erin and brushed her wild hair till it was nearly neat. Fred was sleepy, so he crawled under Ben's bed to rest.

"Are you sure you don't want to come?" Nim asked, but Fred just blinked and went back to sleep.

Her shoulders felt light and empty without him, but it made blending in easier.

This was important because after the dinner with the other Klub Kids, Nim was going to spend the night in Ben and Erin's cabin.

"Your dad doesn't mind you sleeping over?" their mom asked.

"No," said Nim, because it didn't seem as if Jack minded about her at all, and if he did, he'd probably rather she slept in a cabin than on the floor of a boat.

Erin loaned her some pajamas and they squashed into the bed together. Fred stayed under Ben's bed. Nim didn't know if it was to say goodbye to Ben or because he was just too pooped to move.

They talked and talked. None of them wanted to think about tomorrow, but there was still plenty to talk about. Mr. and Mrs. Caritas came in to say good night.

"Don't talk too late," Mr. Caritas said. "It's a big day to-morrow. Do you live in New York, Nim?"

"No," said Nim. "It'll be my first visit."

"You'll love it! But for us vacation is over: we'll be going straight to the airport to fly home."

Their mom bent to kiss Erin on the forehead, and then she kissed Nim too. It felt just like when Alex used to kiss her good night.

Alex! Nim thought into the night, but even in her head she couldn't quite sort out all the things she wanted to say to her, so she sent the wish out in a big jumble of love, sor-riness, and hope.

Ben's voice trickled off into soft snores, but Erin and Nim continued whispering.

The door opened quietly. "You really have to go to sleep now," said Erin's mom, "or Nim will have to go back to her dad."

"That's what you're trying to do!" Erin whispered when the door closed again, and they started to giggle. They gig-gled so hard they had to put the pillows over their heads—and then Erin fell asleep.

Alex heard Nim calling—and then she heard her giggling. She was at the door before she realized she must have been dreaming again.

But it seemed so real!

Nim! she thought into the night, but even in her head she couldn't quite sort out all the things she wanted to say to her, so she sent the wish out in a big jumble of love, sorriness, and hope.

And soon after, Nim stopped worrying and wondering, and fell fast asleep.

16

Nim hugged Erin and Ben goodbye. They'd see each other later, but they wouldn't be able to talk. She gave Ben her green stone and Erin her bamboo cup, which had been in her pocket when she jumped off the cliff. Finally she gave Ben the bird bands, the Troppo Tourist jacket, and, most important of all, the key.

Then she dressed in her own clothes—her bright blue shirt and baggy red pants with drawstring ties and useful pockets—and went down to the Animal Room. She gave the caged animals love and breakfast, trying to let them feel her hope: "You'll all be free soon!"

By nine o'clock there were more butterflies in her stomach than on the Butterfly Deck. It was time for the circus.

The Professor picked up his whip.

"You don't need the whip," Nim said bravely. "Grown-ups won't like it and it will scare the kids."

The Professor flicked a warning crack. "Then you'd better keep those animals under control—because I'll be keeping it close at hand, just in case."

Nim shut her mouth so hard her teeth hurt. It was the

only way to stop herself from calling him every bad name she could think of. She opened the door.

"Selkie, walk!" she ordered. "Fred, follow!"

"Sorry," she whispered as they started down the hall. "After today, I'll *never* talk to you like that again!"

Selkie looked at her with her head on one side and Nim knew she understood, but Fred scuttled along behind looking as cross as an iguana can possibly look.

It was a tight squash in the elevator because none of them wanted to be next to the Professor and his whip. He got out at the Sea Lion Deck, but Nim, Selkie, and Fred went up to the Flamingo Deck above, where the café chairs were set up around the top of the waterslide, as if the deck were a theater balcony for the show at the pool below.

There was a person in every chair, and when Nim looked down she saw people sitting all around the waterslide pool and standing all the way out to the railings. There were more people than Nim had thought could fit on the ship. For a minute she wanted to turn and run. Fred forgot his sulking and scurried to her shoulder.

Then all three friends walked through the café to the top of the waterslide.

Fred rubbed his spiny head under her chin. Nim put her hand on Selkie's shoulder. They were ready. They looked down to see the Professor on a stage beside the pool.

"Ladies and gentlemen!" he shouted. "Instead of my usual lecture this morning, I'll be demonstrating how well I've trained a seal and a lizard—by allowing a mere child to do the show!"

Dozens of kids waved and screamed, "Me! Pick me!"

The Professor ignored them and sat down in a chair on the

stage, his whip across his knees. "This had better be good!" he muttered.

Fred whizzed down the waterslide into the pool. Nim followed—and then Selkie *whoosh*ed down the curves and *whumph*ed! in with a tidal-wave splash. The audience squealed, clapped, and cheered. The people in the front three rows were soaked.

Nim climbed out of the pool to the front stage. She took a deep breath and wondered if her voice would come out at all.

Then she saw Erin and Ben in the very front row—and beside and behind them, all the kids from the Kids' Klub. Suddenly she knew she could do it.

"Ladies and gentlemen!" she shouted. "May I present my sea lion friend, Selkie!"

Selkie pulled herself up on the side of the pool and bowed her head to the left, to the right, and straight ahead. Everyone in the audience felt as if she'd bowed to them.

"And," Nim continued, "the handsomest, funniest, smartest marine iguana in the whole world: Fred!"

Fred had to scramble up the steps and onto Nim's shoulder before he could nod at the audience, but when he did, Erin and Ben cheered so loudly that everyone else had to join in.

"Statue!" Nim shouted, and Selkie sat up as tall and still as the sea lions on the chessboard.

Nim threw four fish and Selkie expertly caught every one. Fred caught lettuce and chunks of fruit.

"Yay, Fred!" the kids all cheered.

Selkie kissed Erin, and Fred sneezed on Ben.

"Yuck, Fred!" the kids all called, laughing as they clapped.

Selkie, Nim, and Fred dived into the pool and played coconut soccer with a ball instead of a coconut.

Now all the audience cheered.

The ship was going slowly down a strait between mainland and islands. High in the distance was a dark speck that just might be a frigate bird.

"Throw the ball here!" the kids all shouted, until the Professor got out of his seat to glare at them.

Nim hopped out of the pool and threw a rubber ring back in. Fred nosed it up from the bottom and Selkie tossed it back.

"Throw something into the pool!" Nim called. "And they'll play catch!"

A boy threw in his watch. "It's waterproof!" he shouted, and the crowd cheered as Selkie tossed it back.

Nim looked at Erin. Erin nodded and threw in a banana.

Fred batted it, Selkie threw it—and Fred gulped it.

"Hooray for Fred!" Kelvin cheered. He still didn't want to touch Fred, but he was glad he'd rescued him.

Out of the corner of her eye, Nim saw Ben slip away from

the crowd and down the stairs, pulling on the Troppo Tourist jacket as he ran.

She also saw that the black speck in the sky had grown into a frigate bird outline.

There was only one fish left in the bucket.

But then Erin pulled out the basket of papier-mâché fish she and Nim had made. She threw the first one to Nim, twirling it high in the air. Nim caught it and threw it the same way to Selkie, who tossed it to Fred, who tossed it back to Nim as Erin threw the next one to Selkie.

The Professor stood up to take a picture, his whip tucked under his arm.

Nim threw the fish to him.

The crowd gasped as an enormous black bird, wings as wide across as the Professor was tall, swooped in to snatch the papier-mâché fish. The Professor gasped and ducked as the bird's left wing brushed his face and its head went through the loop of the dangling whip.

"Introducing Galileo!" Nim shouted, throwing him the last real fish for a reward.

Galileo dropped the papier-mâché fish onto the Professor's head, caught the real one, and soared upward with the whip bouncing on his bright red chest—till it slipped away and sank into the cold waters of New York Harbor.

The Professor bellowed with rage. He was so angry he

forgot to even pretend that he was in charge of the show.

"If you planned this . . . ," he screamed at Nim.

Selkie leapt up and smashed down so hard in front of him that the front rows got soaked all over again. The Professor was drenched, standing in a puddle of water.

"I'm warning you!" the Professor shrieked.

"Play nicely, Selkie!" said Nim, and threw her the ball again.

Selkie leapt up as she hit the ball back, straight and hard at the Professor. He threw his arms up to catch it, skidded in the puddle of water, and fell down hard on his bottom.

Fred scurried to Selkie's head and sneezed in the Professor's face.

The audience laughed and cheered louder than ever, as if it were a clown act.

"Naughty Selkie!" Nim said lovingly. "Naughty Fred!"

"Yuck, Fred!" the kids shouted gleefully.

Selkie *whuffle*d and put her flippers up to her face as if she was crying.

The audience cheered louder.

The Professor's eyes went narrow and his face was purple-red. "That's the end of the show!" he shouted.

Now the ship was going under a bridge. The land was close enough that they could see the cubes and rectangles of buildings, but there was still a bit farther to go.

"Encore!" shouted Erin.

The whole audience took it up. "Encore, encore! More, more, more!"

Nim blew her shell whistle. Selkie pulled herself out of the pool. Fred scrambled up beside her.

"I said the show is over!" the Professor screamed.

"Encore, encore!" the audience screamed back.

Selkie and Fred climbed onto the stage.

Nim blew her whistle again. Selkie dived in, rolling and porpoising around the pool, as if she were loosening up for the swim of her life. Nim dived in and Selkie dived under her so that Nim was riding on her back.

Nim blew the whistle again and Fred dived too, right onto Selkie's back and up to Nim's shoulder.

The audience cheered, the Professor glowered, and Nim, Selkie, and Fred climbed out of the pool.

The ship slowed down still more.

The Professor moved toward Nim. His eyes were as narrow and glinting as a knife. "These animals are going back to their cages," he snarled. "Get into the elevator."

Nim, Selkie, and Fred headed toward it, very, very slowly.

"Wait!" Erin screamed. "I want to pat Selkie goodbye!"

"And Fred!"

"We want to pat Selkie!"

"Me too, me too!"

The kids swarmed around them, patting Selkie and Fred and hugging Nim. Some of the adults joined in, and a few who couldn't get close handed Erin some money to give to Nim. "That show deserves a good tip!" said one soaking-wet woman.

Erin shoved the money into Nim's extra-safe pocket, then whispered something to the little pigtailed girl from the Kids' Klub. The girl ran to the Professor and tagged him on the back. "Spider!" she shouted.

Then Erin and Nim jumped into the elevator.

As the doors shut, Nim saw the mob of kids squeal and surge toward the left-hand rail, with the Professor spluttering and bellowing in the middle of them, locked in as firmly as if in a cage.

Nim pushed the button for the Dolphin Deck, the lowest level with an outside deck. The elevator stopped.

"Ready?" asked Erin.

Nim couldn't speak. She nodded.

Erin burst out of the doors and raced to the left-hand side of the ship. "The Statue of Liberty!" she screamed. "Look at all the birds around the Statue of Liberty!"

There weren't many passengers down on this deck, and most were already staring out over the left-hand side at the great green statue. Now everyone turned too, as an amazing flock of brightly colored birds—parrots, rainbow doves, flamingos, eagles, and toucans, all led by an enormous black frigate bird—came soaring into the blue sky and began wheeling around the torch in the statue's uplifted hand.

Not a single person looked to the other side. If they had, they might have seen a sea lion and a girl with an iguana on her shoulder slip out of the elevator to the right-hand side of the ship.

So they all missed the most spectacular trick of all, the one where Selkie flopped onto a deck chair against the railing and pulled herself into her best-ever flipper-stand. They missed seeing Fred climb on her flippers and be launched from his own personal diving board when Selkie dived over the ship's rail and down, down, down into the water of New York Harbor.

And they missed seeing Nim take the biggest breath of her life—and jump.

17

THE WATER WAS COLDER than ice
cream. Nim gasped as she sank deep
and swirling in the waves of the ship's
huge wake—but then Selkie was below her, strong and solid,
nudging her up through the murky gray.

Nim spluttered out cold water and breathed in warmer air
as Fred scrambled onto her shoulder. She settled herself on
Selkie's back and wrapped her arms around the sea lion's neck.
The ship was already far ahead of them. Selkie could swim
fast, but she had to move slowly with Nim on her back. They
still had a long way to go.

To the left they could see the statue of an enormous green
woman with birds circling her torch. Beside her was a small island with square red-brick buildings. Straight ahead was the
huge city-island Nim and her friends were trying to reach: an
island covered with shining gray towers as tall as the ship was
long. It was as different from Nim's island as any place in the
world could be.

"You," Alex said to herself when she woke up, "are the

most mixed-up, muddleheaded, woolly-witted woman in the world."

Alex agreed.

"You were living in a paradise with people you love, and you ran away."

"It's the worst thing I've ever done," Alex agreed.

"So what are you going to do about it, Alex?"

"Go back," said Alex. "Go straight back, figure things out, and make them right again."

"You'll go straight to the airport when you get off the ship?"

Alex thought for a second. "First I'll go to see Delia."

Halfway around the world, Jack was fast asleep, stretched out behind a row of chairs on the Isla Grande airport floor. It wasn't much more comfortable than the raft, but Jack didn't want to leave the airport and miss the plane. He didn't want anything to keep him from finding Nim and Alex.

Back in New York Harbor, Nim and her friends found themselves surrounded by boats. There were three ships ahead of the Troppo Tourists, boxy orange ferries, small bright yellow water taxis, sleek yachts, and more than a dozen sailboats. Small planes darted overhead, and a helicopter whirred so fiercely that Selkie forgot about Nim and dove down deep. Nim and Fred floated off in surprise. Suddenly the waves seemed higher and the current seemed stronger—and Nim was colder and more tired than she'd ever been.

"Selkie!" she shouted. "Come back!"

Selkie glided up from below, *whuffl*ing apologetically as Nim and Fred slid back on.

The closer the buildings got, the bigger they grew. They were as tall as mountains, and they covered the island so thickly Nim wondered how people could walk in between them.

A motorboat roared by. Selkie swerved out of its way, but now two sailboats were following, with a whole fleet of other sailboats chasing them and a water taxi zipping through the middle.

"We've got to get out of here!" Nim said.

Selkie veered to the right, away from the racing sailboats.

A little gray-and-white tugboat with red trim and a fat and friendly shape was coming their way. No matter which way Selkie veered, the tug kept coming straight toward them. Its engines were slowing, and there was a man standing at the bow waving while another rushed to unclip its round white life rings.

"Hang on!" the captain shouted from a loudspeaker in the wheelhouse. "We're coming!"

Nim and Selkie had been friends since Nim was a toddler. They both knew what the other was feeling, and now they both knew that they would never get to shore without help.

"If they try to put us in jail, we'll just have to escape again!" Nim told Selkie and Fred, trying to sound braver than she felt.

The men tossed out the life rings. Then the youngest man threw off his jacket and shoes and jumped in. Nim slipped off Selkie, Fred slipped off Nim, and they all swam toward the boat.

"Over here!" shouted one of the men, running to the tug's low, flat back section. "Daniel, bring her around to the stern!"

"Right!" the young man shouted, swimming desperately toward Nim. "Don't worry! I'm coming!"

With Daniel on one side and Selkie on the other, Nim swam to the tug.

The two men on deck threw themselves down, reaching over the side to Nim. She grabbed their arms and was pulled up on board. Daniel followed.

Nim was coughing, spluttering, and shaking, and her teeth were chattering so hard she could barely speak. "Please get Fred!"

Daniel rushed to the edge. "There's someone else out there?"

Nim pointed. Fred was riding on top of one of the life rings.

"That's Fred?" Daniel asked. He was shivering a bit too. "I guess he can't hang on to the life ring if we pull it in?"

Nim shook her head.

"Well," said Daniel, readying himself to jump in again, "I sure hope he appreciates this."

But at that moment, Selkie came up under Fred and soccer-tossed him onto the deck. Then, with a mighty heave, she flopped up beside him.

The older man came back from the wheelhouse with a blanket and wrapped it snugly around Nim. "I take it they're friends of yours?" he asked as Fred scurried to Nim's shoulder and Selkie settled herself protectively behind them.

Nim nodded.

"Okay. Because otherwise that's one lost sea lion, let alone the iguana. So what happened?"

"I fell off a boat," Nim said, pointing vaguely toward the disappearing sailboats.

"You fell off a boat and nobody noticed?"

Nim nodded, her teeth still chattering.

"Hmm. That's not the whole story, is it?"

"No," Nim said honestly.

"Well, let's get you warmed up and we'll work out what to do with you. How about some hot chocolate? And, Daniel, you're the skinniest—how about finding her a spare T-shirt so we can dry her clothes?"

Nim went into the cabin and changed into Daniel's T-shirt. It came down to her knees like a dress, so she could hang her own clothes out over the line to dry in the sun.

"Now," said the older man when Nim reappeared. "Let's start with names. You can call me Ivan. And you are . . . ?"

"Nim Rusoe."

"And where are your parents, Miss Nim Rusoe? Who am I going to call to say we've fished you out of the harbor and could they please come and pick you up?"

"My mom's dead," said Nim, "and you can't call my dad. But I'm looking for my grown-up friend Alex Rover."

"Alex Rover, like the author?" asked Ivan.

"Nim, like *Nim's Island?*" asked Daniel, pointing to a water taxi zipping toward the shore. On its side was an enormous poster of a girl with a spyglass at her eye and an iguana on her shoulder, leaning out from the top of a palm tree while a sea lion splashed in the cove below. NIM'S ISLAND was written around the top, and "the newest by ALEX ROVER" in even bigger letters underneath.

Nim's brain couldn't believe what her eyes were seeing. It was like looking into her rainwater pool and seeing a strange, almost-Nim reflection looking back at her.

"Yes," she whispered. "That's me."

18

JACK CHECKED HIS E-MAIL at the airport again before his flight left. There was still nothing from Alex or Nim. Before, Jack hadn't known if he was more scared or angry. Now he knew: he was just plain scared. Because it didn't make sense: Alex would never have taken Nim without telling him. And Nim would never leave without telling him.

But what else could have happened? What if they'd been kidnapped by the supply plane pilot? What if he'd come right across the world to find them and they were still somewhere near the island? Should he jump straight onto a plane home the instant he landed?

I've got this far, he decided. *I'll look for them in the city first.*

But as the plane roared up the runway, Jack suddenly remembered that if someone's name wasn't in his address book, the message went into the Trash folder unless it had the words "science" or "research" in the subject line.

Alex and Nim didn't know that.

And the Trash folder had blinked every time he'd checked his e-mails.

Why didn't I check? Jack thought. *There could be a message about them in the Trash folder right now!*

But he'd have to wait till the plane landed before he could find out.

Ivan was just about to phone Delia Defoe to tell her about Nim when a call came in over their radio. A big cruise ship needed a tugboat to tow it up the Hudson River to its dock.

"I guess we could take you with us," said Ivan. "Maybe someone could meet you at the cruise ship terminal."

"No!" Nim exclaimed. "I can't go anywhere near the cruise ships!"

Ivan looked at her shrewdly. "You might have to tell us a bit more of your story, young Nim."

"There's a professor on the ship. He kidnapped Selkie, and he wanted Fred too. He said that was the law because of the Foundation for Research on Intelligent, Unique, and Interesting Animals—but Selkie's been my friend since I was three, and Fred since he was hatched . . . they can't belong to this Foundation and get taken away to be studied. They just can't."

"So you jumped overboard to save them?"

Nim nodded.

Daniel whistled.

"Well," said Ivan, "you've got the courage of your convictions, that's for sure. I don't see that we've got any choice but to get you where you're going, sea lion, iguana, and all. And until the police have looked into this professor and his Foundation, we'll help you steer clear of him."

"We could drop you off somewhere," Daniel suggested, "if someone could meet you."

Ivan phoned Papyrus Publishing. When he asked to speak to Delia Defoe, he was put through to her voice mail. And when he phoned back and tried to explain that he had the real Nim with him and that she needed to find Alex Rover, he was put through to a special recorded announcement about publicity for Alex Rover's new book. When he tried a third time and explained how urgent it was, he was told that Papyrus Publishing never, ever gave out an author's address or phone number.

"I'm afraid you'll simply have to go to the publishing house," said Ivan. "We could put you in a cab."

"I don't think a cab would take Selkie," Daniel pointed out.

"But I can't leave Selkie!" Nim protested.

"*Ork!*" Selkie barked.

"I know!" said Daniel. "I'll phone my sister-in-law, Carla. You'll all fit in her delivery van."

He picked up his phone. Nim could faintly hear Carla on the other end: "A sea lion? Are you for real?"

The radio crackled. "The cruise ship's waiting. Is there a problem?"

Daniel grinned as he put away his phone. "We're in luck— Carla's down near the water taxi dock right now."

"Give me five minutes!" Ivan said into the radio. "We've got an emergency delivery to the water taxi dock."

"Does Carla like sea lions?" Nim asked anxiously.

"Sure! She's just never met one."

"And marine iguanas?"

"Who wouldn't love Fred?"

Fred smirked and went on munching the salad Ivan had made for him.

Nim's clothes were nearly dry. She took them off the line and changed in the cabin as they pulled in to the dock.

Ivan handed her a card when she came back to the wheelhouse. "Now, Miss Nim Rusoe, you'll be fine with Carla. But this has got my name and phone number—you call me if you've got any problems. You call me if you don't have any problems! We want to hear you got there safe."

"Thank you," said Nim. "And thank you for the sandwich and hot chocolate." If she ever did get back to the island, she thought, maybe she could take some hot chocolate with her.

"Here's my number too," said Daniel.

"And thank you for rescuing me," Nim said.

"Anyone jumps off a ship into the Hudson River to rescue their friends," said Daniel, "I'd be proud to pull them out."

"Just don't make a habit of it!" Ivan warned, giving her a warm hug. "And don't forget to call us."

The tug bumped up against the dock. Daniel jumped down, and Selkie, Nim, and Fred followed him to the edge of a park, with a wide stretch of green grass that ended at a path as smooth and hard as rock. The path was so crowded that everyone had to move fast and determinedly. Nim had never imagined that so many people could fit into the same place at the same time.

While they walked, they talked on phones, to each other, or to themselves. Some used words Nim couldn't understand and languages she'd never heard. They drank cans of soda and cups of coffee, ate ice cream on sticks and hot dogs and pretzels, carried purses and briefcases and fat bags with shopping or small dogs inside—and somehow they hardly ever bumped into each other!

"Come on," said Daniel. "Carla's waiting. It'll be fine."

Nim took a deep breath. Fred curled himself tighter around her neck. Selkie pressed hard against her. They followed Daniel down the path.

Next to the path was a road, and on the road there were cars. Lots of yellow cars, and lots of every-other-color-in-the-world cars. Some were going one way and some were going the other, but just when Nim thought they'd meet *smash* in the middle, they slipped safely on by.

Nim had seen pictures of cars, but she'd never heard the noise or smelled the smell. The smell was hot and the noise was hotter, and just when she thought it couldn't get any louder, there was a high-pitched siren and a roaring noise like a sea lion bull, and a huge red truck came screaming by.

Selkie didn't like this place with all its strange noises, and

she wanted to get out of it as fast as she could. She galumphed off the path onto the street.

Cars *honk*ed and brakes screeched.

"Selkie!" shouted Nim, dashing into the road after her.

"Wait!" shouted Daniel, grabbing Nim's arm.

"What part of DON'T WALK don't you understand?" shouted a driver in a yellow car at the people dashing across while the cars stopped for Selkie.

Selkie barked crossly and flopped back up onto the path.

"It's Nim and the sea lion!" shouted a woman on the opposite side of the road.

"Is that who you're supposed to be?" a man called. "Are you supposed to be Nim?"

"Great publicity stunt!" cheered another man.

Then the cars stopped, and so did the flashing sign of a red warning hand. As everyone stepped onto the street, the sign below lit up to show a little man walking.

So that's how they know when to do it! thought Nim, and stepped up onto the sidewalk on the other side.

They hurried on through a little park, ignoring the flowers and cool splashing fountain. At the end of the park was an enormous bull.

Selkie barked and wouldn't go on.

"It's okay!" Nim coaxed. "He's just a statue!"

Selkie froze into her statue trick, and the people who were lined up to have their pictures taken with the bull ran over to take pictures of Selkie too.

"Is that a real sea lion?"

"Is it safe?"

"Of course," said Nim, and a woman rushed up to stand beside her while her friend took a picture. Fred reached over and gulped the top off her ice cream cone.

"Sorry," said Nim, though Fred wasn't sorry at all.

There was a whisper of excitement, and more people kept coming and taking more pictures.

"Got to keep moving, guys!" Daniel said.

"Where are you going?" a long-haired man called.

"Papyrus Publishing."

"Do you need the address?" asked a grandmotherly woman, writing it on the back of her shopping list. "My son works there."

"That's a long way uptown," said a woman in a red suit. "How're you going to get them there?"

"You could take the subway!" suggested the long-haired man.

"You can't take a sea lion on the subway!" said the red-suited woman. "You'd need to call one of those cabs that take dogs."

"My sister uses those to take her dogs to day care," said a carpenter walking past. "I'll call her and get their number."

"Thanks," said Daniel, "but we've already got a ride." They crossed the avenue to a woman opening the back door of a van covered with pictures of dogs and the words CARLA'S CANINE CAKES.

19

CARLA KISSED DANIEL, hugged Nim, patted Selkie, and almost patted Fred—all at once and all while she was talking. "Glad to help out. I thought Daniel must be kidding, but you're for real, all right! You can tell me your story on the way—where is it you need to go?"

Daniel gave her Papyrus Publishing's address, ruffled Nim's hair, and jogged back to the dock where the tugboat was waiting.

"We've got to do a few deliveries on the way," said Carla. "The cakes can't wait! I've stacked up the boxes so the sea lion can fit—Selkie, is it? Selkie, can you hop right in there, honey? Just don't squish the boxes!"

Selkie flopped into the back of the van, in front of the

stacked cake boxes. It was cool, and if she sat up high she'd be able to see out the back window. She gave a *honk* of approval.

"And what about this little guy?" Carla asked, pointing to Fred. "He's not going to climb all over the boxes, is he?"

"He might," said Nim.

"Okay, Fred, in the front with Fritz. And you too, Nim. Fritz, stop barking. I'm sure Fred's much nicer than he looks. Buckle up and off we go; we've got a bunch of cakes to get where they're going."

Fritz was a dachshund, a short-legged, long-bodied dog about the same size and shape as Fred. At first he squeezed himself against Carla, but then he wiggled up against Nim. Fred glared fiercely, and Fritz crawled across Nim to the side window so he could stand and look out, carefully ignoring Fred.

Fred did the same, carefully ignoring Fritz.

A bus went by. It was completely covered by the same *Nim's Island* picture as the water taxi.

Carla laughed. "Would you look at that! How do you feel about people staring at you all over Manhattan?"

"A bit strange," said Nim, because it seemed more polite than saying it made her stomach squirm like a tangle of worms.

"So?" asked Carla. "Spill the story. What's a kid doing in New York City all on her lonesome? Or to put it another way, what's a kid doing with a sea lion and an iguana and their picture on a bus? You know, I see a lot of strange things driving around this town, but I've never seen that before. Now, where did I put the address for that Dalmatian cake? There it is, under your feet. Just grab it for me, will you?"

A yellow car with a *Nim's Island* sign on the back blared its horn.

"Hey!" Carla shouted back. "I've got the real thing in here, so just watch who you're *honk*ing at!"

Fritz barked in agreement. Fred stared fiercely. Nim began to tell her story.

"Here we are!" Carla exclaimed a few minutes later, turning into a side street and stopping with a jolt. "We'll have to get Selkie out so I can reach the cake . . . will you guys be okay while I run it up? It's only half a block, twelfth floor, this says—won't take me more than ten minutes."

"We'll be fine," said Nim—but Selkie had seen a pond.

It was a wide, shallow pond in a small park, with a splashing fountain in the middle. Two boys and a girl were standing by the fountain, and a mother and her toddler were slapping at the shallow water at the pond's edge. Selkie galumphed down the sidewalk, went through a big marble arch, and cannonballed in. The pond was even shallower than she'd realized, and instead of sinking down she skidded right across to the other side.

The toddler laughed and clapped his hands. His mother whisked him up and stood, ready to run.

"She won't hurt him!" Nim called, jogging across with Fred and Fritz close behind.

"Okay," said the mom, and after a while she put the toddler down again to splash and watch Selkie.

Selkie rolled on her back and Nim splashed water over her dusty belly. Fred waded across to the fountain. Fritz followed him, till Fred climbed into the jet of spray so that it bubbled up to tickle his tummy.

"Cool!" said one of the boys.

"Is he yours?" asked the other.

"And the sea lion?" asked the girl.

"They're my friends," said Nim.

"Do you belong to a circus?"

"We don't belong to anyone," said Nim. "We're just us."

But now she could see Carla crossing the street back toward the park. "Fred!" she called. "Selkie! Fritz! Time to get going!"

The kids ran back to the van with them, waving goodbye as they drove off.

• • •

Alex saw the Statue of Liberty out her cabin window as the ship sailed past. She had nothing to pack but the pajamas and toothbrush she'd bought and the book that Delia had sent her.

For the first time, she opened her new book and began to read.

The ship gradually slowed to nearly a full stop. The engines were barely purring. There seemed to be quite a long wait before a tugboat towed it to the dock.

Alex began to smile as she read.

The ship docked. Ropes were run out and looped over the bollards on the dock; the gangplank slammed down.

Alex looked up, wishing she were reading the book aloud to Jack and Nim, with Fred, Selkie, and Chica looking on.

People were walking past her window, wheeling suitcases and carrying backpacks.

The mother of the next-door children called, "I asked you to pack this morning!"

The children shouted, "We were going to! But we had tons of other things to do!"

Alex went on reading.

Virginia knocked on the door to tell her it was time to leave the ship and ask if she needed help with her bags.

"No thanks," said Alex, and went to stand in line to say goodbye to the crew. She went on reading as she stood.

She shook hands with the captain and saw that the family in the cabins next door had lined up behind her. The children looked as bouncy and friendly as they'd sounded through the walls, and Alex wished she'd been brave enough to meet them. She joined an even longer line to show her passport and leave the dock—and very nearly finished her book.

"I do know the ending," she reminded herself. "At least I think I do."

Suddenly she could hardly wait to get off the ship and sort out the ending to her even newer story.

"Do you see that woman's book?" Ben asked Erin.

Erin stared hard. A nasty little shock went through her as she read the title. "Do you think Nim just read it and made everything up?"

"She couldn't have. She had Fred."

"And Selkie."

"It's still very weird."

"What's even weirder is that woman's wearing pants like Nim's. *Nobody* has pants like Nim's."

"And she hasn't got a suitcase."

"As if she got on in a hurry . . ."

". . . like Nim."

"Do you think it could be?"

"Let's ask her!"

But by the time all their passports were stamped and bags checked, Alex had vanished.

Ben and Erin followed their parents and the twins out to stand in line for a taxi. The first one to pull in had a sign on the roof: **NIM'S ISLAND** BY ALEX ROVER: IN STORES JULY 14!

"That's today," said Erin.

"So the only person on the ship who could already be reading it . . ."

". . . is Alex Rover!"

Ben started to giggle. "Can you imagine what she'll say when she sees Nim!"

"And Selkie and Fred!"

Jack's plane didn't go all the way to New York; he had to change planes twice. He rushed to check his e-mail again at

an airport computer as he waited for the last plane. This time he went straight to the Trash folder. It was crammed with messages.

As he skimmed down the list, his heart started *thump*ing so fast he could hardly breathe.

To: jack.rusoe@explorer.net
From: erin@kidmail.com
Date: Wednesday 14 July, 11:30 a.m.
Subject: Very very urgent about Nim
Dear Mr. Rusoe,
I'm the girl who sent Nim's e-mails to you before. I hope you don't think I'm rude, but I think it's very mean that you haven't written to Nim yet. Anyway, I thought you'd like to know that the ship's in New York now and it's going to dock in about half an hour. We're getting off at the cruise ship terminal, but Nim and Selkie and Fred jumped off when everyone was looking at the Statue of Liberty.

"Jumped off the ship?" Jack exclaimed.

Nim didn't ask me to write to you this time, but I hope it's okay because she's worried that you're angry at her about Alex, and she's my friend so I don't

151

want her to be upset, so could you please write to her soon? I guess she can check her e-mail when she finds Alex.

From Erin Caritas

Jack felt hot and cold at the same time. He read the e-mail over and over, even though every word was already burned into his brain, especially "jumped off" and "when she finds Alex."

Then he went down through all the e-mails that had been in the Trash folder every time he'd checked for mail from Nim or Alex.

He found all five messages that Nim had asked Erin to write. When he'd finished reading, he knew that:

Nim, Selkie, and Fred had jumped off a ship in the middle of
    New York Harbor about two hours ago.

They weren't with Alex.

There were lots more things that he didn't know, but the most important were:

Did Nim, Selkie, and Fred drown when they jumped off the
    ship?

If they hadn't drowned, where were they now?

Where was Alex?

The other things he really wanted to know but would worry about later were:

Why did they get onto the ship?

How did they get onto the ship?

When did they get onto the ship?

Why did Alex leave?

But the most important question of all he couldn't even ask because no one knew the answer: Would they all be able to find each other?

To: erin@kidmail.com

From: jack.rusoe@explorer.net

Date: Wednesday 14 July, 1:01 p.m.

Subject: re: Very very urgent about Nim

Dear Erin,

Do you really mean that Nim jumped off a ship and swam to land?

I'm arriving in New York 6:00 this afternoon on Flight 123. If you talk to Nim, please tell her.

I'm very sorry I didn't read your e-mails before.

Yours truly,

Jack Rusoe

P.S. Thank you for being Nim's friend.

He started another e-mail.

To: aka@incognito.net

The airport loudspeaker crackled. "Passenger Jack Rusoe, please go to the boarding gate immediately. Your flight is about to leave."

Jack left the computer and raced to the gate. *Five more hours till I'm there!* he thought.

It was going to be the longest five hours of his life.

20

CARLA DROVE NIM and her friends past old buildings, new buildings, buildings of carved stone, buildings of shiny glass, and building after building whose top was high above the clouds. None of them were where Alex's books were published.

How would I ever have found Delia by myself? Nim wondered. *And if I couldn't find her, how would I ever find Alex?*

They passed banks, dress stores, camera stores, jewelry stores, postcard stores, hotels, cafés, and stands on the street corners selling handbags or sunglasses or snacks and drinks. They saw flags waving, neon signs flashing, stairs going down into the ground, and steam hissing up from a hole in the street, the way it did from the Hissing Stones when Fire Mountain was getting angry.

They stopped at traffic lights and watched the people crossing. "Isn't it funny," Nim said, "there are so many people—and none of them are ever the same!"

"That's what makes life interesting, honey," said Carla. "But what I want to see right now is the apartment waiting for this poodle birthday cake. Don't yap, Fritz, poodles are nice too. Let's see, if I turn here, go down this street, and now . . .

oh dear, that was exactly what I didn't want to do. Okay, we're going to have to park here and walk. You guys can hop out and stretch if you want. Better put Fritz on his leash—has Fred got a leash?"

"He'll go on my shoulder," said Nim, because the sidewalks were even more crowded here.

"Okay, don't go far. I'll be quick as I can." Carla opened the back of the van to let Selkie out, grabbed the cake box, and raced off. Nim and the others followed more slowly, with Selkie pressed close to Nim's side.

On the corner a man was selling pretzels. The pretzels were like bread twisted into knots and were covered with salt. Fred liked salt. He leaned out from Nim's shoulder and chomped half a pretzel from the stand.

"That'll be one dollar!" said the man.

I don't have any money! Nim thought—but then she remembered the tips from the show that Erin had dropped into her pocket as they got into the elevator. She showed them to the pretzel seller.

"Too much!" he said, taking one green piece and giving her back the rest. Nim bought a bottle of water too, and she still had money left.

They crossed the road, turned the corner—and walked into a solid wall of people. Most of them tried to jump out of Selkie's way, though they were too jammed in to jump far.

There were giant computerized screens on the fronts of buildings on both sides of the street. Some of the screens had pictures that changed from one thing to another and back again; others had brightly lit words running across them, starting over again as soon as they'd finished.

One of the running signs proclaimed: ALEX ROVER'S NIM'S ISLAND RELEASED TODAY.

Nim felt as if the only things that were real were the feel of Fred's spine under her chin and the warmth of Selkie's shoulder.

"Let's go back to the van," she said, but now it was hard to turn around.

"*Whoof!*" Selkie barked. "*Whoof-WHOOF!*"

The crowd shifted just enough for Nim to get through—but then some people noticed Selkie and crowded closer to see.

"They're from Alex Rover's new book!"

"They must be filming a movie!"

More people crushed closer against Nim and her friends.

A policeman whistled. Selkie stopped, but the whistle wasn't for her. It was to make the cars stop so Selkie and Nim could cross, with a long parade following behind.

"Where are we going?" a girl asked.

"Back to Carla's van," said Nim. "And then to find Alex Rover."

"We're on TV!" shrieked a boy, leaping in front of Nim to wave to a man walking backward with a camera on his shoulder.

Some people stopped following, but some came closer to ask about Alex. One man pushed his way through with a pen and a book and asked Nim to sign it. It was Alex's book—and even though looking at it made Nim feel sorry, ashamed, and confused, when she read Alex's name she felt a tiny trickle of hope that maybe Alex would still like her after all.

The man kept on asking till Nim scribbled her name across the face of the girl who was supposed to be her.

"Can I have your autograph too?" a boy asked, but just as other people started pulling out pieces of paper, notebooks, and pens, Fred sneezed. Hard.

And everyone stepped back.

Fred looked very pleased with himself as they met Carla and started off again. The van crawled through the traffic. "We're nearly there," Carla explained. "What we're going to do is loop around, drop off this dog-that-looks-like-a-cat cake—stop yapping, Fritz, though you're right, who'd want a dog that looks like a cat? But this customer asked for it, so that's what she's getting, and then we'll get Nim where she needs to be."

Carla turned where the road met a wide green park. Nim saw soft grass, flowers, tall trees, and hills. It was like the fresh green heart of this hot, busy city.

In the park, people walked and dreamed, lay on the grass, jogged, rollerbladed, and rode bikes and horses. There were mothers with babies, fathers with toddlers, grandparents with grandchildren, more mothers and fathers with little kids and big kids and almost grown-up kids.

Families! thought Nim, and suddenly she didn't want to see any more.

Carla parked in a row of horses and carriages in front of a hotel that looked like a palace. "Don't go away!" Carla said, letting them all out again to get the dog-that-looked-like-a-cat cake. "I'll just be a minute!"

Selkie *honk*ed in surprise at the horses. She'd never seen animals with such long legs. A big gray horse whinnied back, and Selkie lolloped over to meet it. "You're a long way from home!" the driver said to Selkie. "It's a good thing Mabel likes tourists." He rubbed the horse's neck affectionately.

Mabel and Selkie sniffed noses. Fred and Fritz gulped some popcorn they'd found on the ground.

Nim tried to enjoy the horses and carriages, the golden fountain, the palace, the brilliant sunshine, and the green park. But soon she'd be at Alex's publisher, and if Delia Defoe couldn't help her, she had no idea at all what she was going to do next.

Carla bustled back, looking flushed and cross. "Turns out they wanted two cakes! Would have been nice if they'd told me when they ordered! So I'm thinking . . . do you want to go back to the shop with me, and then I can go in to find this Delia with you?"

But Nim couldn't wait any longer. "We can go in by ourselves," she said, though she was suddenly more afraid than she'd been ever since she stood at the railing to dive off the ship.

"Okay, then . . . you didn't think I was dumping you off for good? I'll just be about an hour—plenty of time to find out if this Delia gal can help you. Then I'll come back and see what's happening, and you can all come and stay with me till you find your friend or your dad or whoever."

"We can stay with you?" Nim asked, amazed.

"Well, I'm hardly going to let you sleep out in Central Park! For one thing, Daniel would never speak to me again. Though I warn you, at my house, it'll be a squish."

Nim tried to say thank you, but her throat was even more choked now than when she'd been afraid. Her new friend got them all back in the van and began driving away from the horses and the hotel.

"Here we are!" Carla pulled up in front of a tall, shining building with Alex Rover's name hung in a banner across a window display of *Nim's Island* books. She gave Nim a card, hugged her hard, and patted Fred before opening the back door for Selkie. "Here's my number in case you need it. Remember, I'll be back in an hour."

She pulled back into the traffic, sticking her head out the window to shout, "Don't worry!"

"I won't," Nim lied, and waved goodbye.

Nim pushed the heavy glass door, and when she stepped in, another door followed close behind, so there was only just enough space for her and Fred. Selkie threw herself at the second slot so hard that all the doors spun around, and Nim ended up back on the street where she'd begun.

Nim tried again. This time they all got into the building.

Books in glass cases were on every side, up to the ceiling. Nim knew she was in the right place.

Three men were sitting behind a desk.

"Oh my goodness!" said the first.

"You'd think Publicity could have told us about this!" said the second.

"Let me guess," said the third. "You must be Nim!"

"Yes," said Nim. "I need to see Alex Rover."

The men looked at each other.

"Get Delia Defoe," said one, and the second man picked up the phone.

"Wait there, sweetie," said the third, and Nim and Selkie sat down in front of the bookcases. Nim read the titles while Fred and Selkie watched the people coming in and going out through the heavy revolving door.

Elevator doors opened, and a woman stepped out.

"I'm Alex Rover's editor," she said. "I appreciate your interest in this book—and I'm very intrigued about how you organized these animals so fast—but Alex Rover doesn't give interviews."

"I don't want an interview," said Nim. "I just have to talk to her."

"Most people think Alex Rover's a man—how did you know she's a woman?"

"Because she's my friend," said Nim. "Or she was."

"Well, I could give her your message. Why do you need to see her?"

"To say I'm sorry," Nim muttered, hiding her face against her knees so Delia wouldn't see her cry.

"Do you mean," Delia said softly, as if she couldn't quite believe what she was asking, "that you're the real Nim? And this is truly Fred, and Selkie?"

Nim nodded.

Delia squatted down on the floor beside her, and Nim told her the story—everything except exactly what she'd said to Alex, because she thought Delia wouldn't want to help her if she knew just how horrible Nim had been.

At first Delia looked excited, but as the story went on, she looked more and more concerned.

"So now can you tell me how to find Alex?" asked Nim.

"I'd love to," said Delia. "The problem is—I don't have any idea."

21

WHEN ALEX FINALLY GOT out of the terminal building on the pier, she could see the top of her publisher's building, tall and shining with the top hidden in the clouds. There was a long line for taxis, and Alex needed to get there fast. She crossed the highway and started to walk.

She wrote her e-mail to Nim and Jack in her head as she walked. The only thing she didn't know was what their answer would be.

She was thinking about them so hard that sometimes she'd see a girl with hair like Nim's, or a man who walked like Jack, and for half a moment she'd think, *They're here!*

It was so bad that when she looked in the window of her publisher's building, she thought she saw Selkie sitting in front of the bookcases.

"You," Alex told herself, "are going absolutely fruitcake nutty!"

"But," she added, "in five more minutes you can e-mail them."

• • •

"First things first," Delia was saying to Nim. "Come up to my office to e-mail Alex and your father—Selkie and Fred can stay down here, can't they?"

Selkie barked and pressed hard against Nim, while Fred scrambled up to her shoulder.

"Okay," said Delia. "I guess we can take the freight elevator."

Suddenly Selkie barked louder and skidded across to the revolving door as fast as she could lollop.

"Selkie!" shouted Nim. And then she saw Alex.

They raced across the floor and met in the middle, hanging on just as tight as they had when Nim pulled Alex out of a sinking sailboat. Selkie *whuffled* around them in a loving circle and Fred climbed up to Alex's shoulder.

"But how?" Alex asked. "And when?"

"On a ship," said Nim. "I'm sorry, I'm so sorry."

"Where's Jack?"

"He's back on the island. But I think he's very mad at me because I made you leave us."

"Do you mean you came *alone?*"

"That's what she means," said Delia. "Which is one of the many reasons I'm so happy to see my bestselling author!"

Alex let go of Nim for just long enough to hug Delia too. "Before we do anything else," she said, "could we please e-mail Jack?"

Delia led them around to the freight elevator and they all rode up to her office, with Nim and Alex still both talking at once and trying to explain.

". . . and then we jumped off," said Nim. "Near the green lady."

"Jumped off what?" asked Alex, feeling stunned.

"The ship," said Nim.

Alex felt as if her heart had stopped. "What ship?" she asked when it started again.

Nim told her, and Alex told Nim her story, and Nim laughed and cried and Alex cried and laughed when they realized that Nim had been hiding right outside Alex's cabin for that whole week.

Then Alex checked her e-mail, and the messages came flooding in. She read through Jack's messages from the last right back to the first. The more she read the paler she got, because Jack was so angry and sad she knew he'd never want to see her again.

"But I told him what happened," Nim said sadly. "Erin sent an e-mail every day."

"Maybe he was too sad to understand?" said Alex.

To: jack.rusoe@explorer.net
From: aka@incognito.net
Date: Wednesday 14 July, 3:32 p.m.
Subject: I've found Alex!!!!
Dear Jack,
You shouldn't be angry at Alex because it's not her fault that I left. It is *my* fault that *she* left.

I wish you could come here too.

We are going down to the sea now so Selkie and Fred can swim in salt water, because they've just been in fountains since we got to the city. I hope your e-mail is working so you get this and I hope you answer.
Love (as much as Selkie loves us),
Nim

"But what if the Professor tries to catch Selkie again?" Nim asked.

"NO ONE is ever going to take Selkie away again!" said Alex. She looked so fierce that Nim believed her.

Delia's phone rang. "There's someone waiting for you downstairs," she said when she'd hung up, and for just a minute both Nim and Alex thought, *Jack!*

They all rode the freight elevator back down to the lobby, and though it wasn't Jack, Nim was still very glad to see Carla, Fred was glad to see Fritz, and Alex and Delia were glad to meet someone who'd helped Nim. There were more thank-yous and more exclaiming and explaining, and then Carla and Fritz dashed off to start baking tomorrow's cakes.

A long white car with black windows pulled up in front. The driver got out to open the doors.

"Here's your car," said Delia. "Are you sure you don't want me to organize a hotel?"

"Thanks," said Alex, "but I'd like to do it myself. It's time I learned to do things like that."

A boy and a girl with their mother stopped to stare as Alex, Delia, Nim and Fred, and finally Selkie came out through the revolving door.

"Look, a sea lion!"

"Hey, that kid's got a lizard on her shoulder!"

"Oh, they're just advertising a book," said the mother.

Nim and Alex looked at each other and laughed so hard

they had to lean against the limousine before they could get into it.

Delia waved goodbye as the car pulled out, with Nim and Alex sitting beside each other, Fred on the back of the seat staring out a window, and Selkie sitting on the floor and staring out hers.

Alex pushed a button in the limousine's door and her window rolled down. Nim pushed the button for Selkie and rolled Fred's down just enough that he could put his head out, but not so far he could fall out by mistake.

"Help yourself to a drink," the driver said.

There were bottles of water in a cupboard behind the driver's seat. Nim poured some into a lid for Fred. Selkie drank hers straight from the bottle.

The limousine driver politely asked Selkie not to put her head out the window with the bottle in her mouth. Selkie finished her water fast: she liked having her head out of the window.

When they stopped at a light, three dogs crossed the road in front of them.

"WHOOF!" honked Selkie, racing from one window to the next.

"*Arf!*" the dogs yipped in surprise.

Selkie *whuffle*d happily. Limousines were much nicer than being on her own in the back of a van, trying not to move in case she squashed cakes.

The driver took them to another park a little farther up the river from where the tugboat had brought Nim that morning. There was a marina, with boats moored all along the wharves: sailboats, motorboats, and some that looked more like floating houses. One had flower boxes at its windows and a FOR LEASE sign on its bow.

"Interesting!" Alex said thoughtfully. "But I'm starving. Let's get something to eat."

Fred rubbed his spiky back against her ankle. He'd nearly forgotten how much he liked Alex.

The four of them walked together across the green grass, back to a café in the middle. They sat at an outside table, where Selkie and Fred could watch the dogs sitting at other tables with their people. Alex ordered fish and chips and salad but added, "One fish needs to be raw, please!"

"Of course!" said the waiter, and brought Selkie and Fred a bowl of water to share while they waited.

"I didn't know there were sea lions in the Hudson River," said the man at the next table.

"We're just visiting," Alex explained.

"And I love your mother-and-daughter outfits!" his wife exclaimed. "Did you make them yourself?"

Alex looked embarrassed. "We're not—"

"Yes," said Nim.

Alex's eyes filled up with tears. "We'll have to find somewhere to check e-mails after dinner," she said—because even though Nim had forgiven her for leaving, she didn't know if Jack would.

"But Selkie and Fred need to swim first," said Nim, and so when they'd finished, they wandered back down to the marina. Selkie and Fred lolloped across the strip of park and into the water—and as they ran, more and more people came to stare.

"Quick!" said Alex, and they raced to the end of a pier where a sign said KAYAKS FOR HIRE.

"Have you kayaked before?" asked the woman in charge.

"Of course!" said Alex.

They climbed in and started to paddle. They were splashing as much water as Selkie in a fountain, but somehow they didn't move very far or very fast.

"Are you sure you've done this before?" Nim asked.

"It might have been in one of my books," said Alex. "I get mixed up!"

22

ERIN AND BEN were at the airport with their family, waiting for the plane to take them the rest of the way home. They were early, the plane was late, and they were bored with waiting. Erin wanted to check her e-mail but there were no computers to do it.

"What's so important it can't wait till we get home?" her dad teased.

Erin thought maybe it was time to tell him. "It's about Nim," she began.

"She's on TV!" shouted Ben.

"Amazing scenes in New York earlier today," said the television news above their heads, "when Times Square played host to a visiting sea lion."

Erin spun around to see Nim, Selkie, and Fred pushing through crowds in the square with the giant computerized screens.

"Originally thought to be a publicity stunt for today's release of Alex Rover's new book, *Nim's Island* . . ."

The camera showed a *Nim's Island* bus.

". . . events have now taken a dramatic turn, with a

spokesman for the Troppo Tourist cruise ship claiming that this girl . . ."

Nim's face filled the screen.

". . . had in fact stowed away and stolen the highly trained, valuable sea lion from their care."

"Liar!" shouted Ben.

"Nim!" shouted a man standing beside them. He was staring up at the screen with shock, relief, and rage all dancing over his face—and he had bright eyes and baggy red pants.

"You're Nim's dad!" shouted Erin.

"Who's Nim?" asked the twins.

The television showed Selkie porpoising around Nim and Alex's kayak.

"Our friend Nim!" Erin and Ben said together.

"You're Erin?" exclaimed Jack.

"And I'm Ben," said Ben.

"Tell me everything!" said Jack.

The camera showed the Professor pointing accusingly. It narrowed in on the tranquilizer gun at his side.

"That's the man who seal-napped Selkie!"

"And the other animals and birds."

"Nim didn't mean to stow away—she was trying to rescue Selkie!"

"We've got to help!"

"Police have been called to recapture the animal," said the reporter.

Jack ran toward the Exit sign.

"Wait!" shouted Mr. Caritas. "I'll come with you!"

"We all will," said Mrs. Caritas.

They raced together through the airport to the long line of yellow taxis parked outside. Jack jumped into the first one with Erin, Ben, and their dad, and Mrs. Caritas and the twins grabbed the one behind.

"This is an emergency," said Jack. "To the kayak pier—as fast as you can!"

"The one on the news?" asked the driver. "With the sea lion?"

"Yes. Please hurry!"

"Gotcha!" said the driver, and pulled out so fast they were knocked back in their seats.

The taxi zigzagged and zipped through the freeway traffic. Jack closed his eyes so he didn't have to see the scenery blurring past, and listened hard to Erin and Ben telling him what had happened on the ship. His face was white; sometimes he looked scared and sometimes he groaned, and sometimes he smiled.

"Nim's never had a kid friend," he said at last. "She's very lucky to have met you two."

"We like her so much," said Erin.

"We've never met anyone like her," said Ben.

"I can believe that," said Jack.

When they told him about seeing Alex in the morning, his face grew even paler and sadder, and he didn't say anything at all.

"Why didn't you tell your mom and me about this before?" Mr. Caritas asked.

"We were afraid. . . ."

"Because the Professor said Nim would go to jail!"

"That's not going to happen!" their father and Jack said together.

They crossed a bridge to reach the central part of the city. The taxi *honk*ed and blared its way through the traffic and down to the pier. They could see the masts of sailing boats and a crowd of people gathered on the shore.

Jack handed a wad of money to the driver, leapt from the cab, and ran.

A policeman stopped him. "Whoa! Stop right there. We've got a wild animal loose."

"But that's my daughter!" said Jack. "The girl, not the sea lion. The sea lion's her friend. They've grown up together."

"And the woman?"

"She's . . . ," said Jack. "Well, she used to be . . . I mean, I know who she is, but I don't know if . . ."

"I see," said the policeman. "But the gentleman over there

informs me that the animal is extremely dangerous if approached by untrained people, so I can't let you past."

"That *gentleman*," said Jack, his face turning scarlet with fury, "is a wildlife poacher. Search his ship and you'll find other animals that need to be rescued. *He's* the only dangerous animal here."

The Professor hadn't noticed Jack. He strode over to the policeman. "We can't wait any longer—that animal needs to be recaptured. I'll just shoot it with a tranquilizer dart."

"You're not going to tranquilize that sea lion!" said Jack.

"Everybody keep calm!" said the policeman.

"And you're certainly not going to tranquilize those people!" Jack shouted.

Erin and Ben, their mother and father, and the twins had snuck behind the crowd to where the kayaks were kept. They were now paddling in tight circles around Selkie.

More people from the crowd followed, until every kayak near the pier was surrounding Selkie, blocking her from the Professor.

A reporter pushed his way up to the policeman, followed by a man in a chauffeur's uniform. "This man says he drove the sea lion down here in his limousine, and it wasn't dangerous at all."

"I'll second that!" shouted Carla, racing across the lawn from her van. "She didn't even nip my delicious cakes."

"I don't know if she *belongs* to anyone," said Daniel, "but I know she loves that little girl, and Nim loves her."

"And I think you'll find," said Ivan, "that this is the wildlife poacher I reported to the police earlier today."

"What do you say to all that?" the reporter demanded, shoving his microphone in the Professor's face.

"I say I'm getting that animal back!" shouted the Professor.

"Put the gun down!" shouted the policeman.

The Professor ignored him and raised his dart gun.

Jack sprang at him.

The policeman sprang too.

Jack and the policeman clunked heads, and their heads clunked the Professor's arm.

"Ow!" screamed the Professor as the tranquilizer dart jabbed his leg. "Ooh," he moaned as the injection went in. He slumped facedown and was asleep before the policeman's handcuffs clamped around his wrists.

"And when you wake up," the policeman told him, "you'll have some questions to answer!"

Jack ran across the grass faster than he'd ever run. He dived into the water and swam straight out. Selkie *honk*ed her happiest *honk* as she dove toward him.

"Jack!" Nim shouted.

"Jack!" Alex whispered.

They reached for him—and their kayak tipped over.

The three of them clung to the upside-down kayak, laughing and hugging, exclaiming and explaining, till Fred poked his face up between them and Selkie *honk*ed anxiously that they needed to get back to shore.

"You're right, Selkie," said Jack. "I think it's time for us all to go home."

"All of us?" asked Nim.

"All of us," said Alex.

23

THERE WERE SO MANY things to organize that they couldn't go back to their island right away. "Besides," said Nim, "there's a lot to see on this island!"

So while Jack and Nim went to talk to the police about the Professor, Alex went to see the boat that looked like a cottage and rented it for two weeks. Selkie and Fred liked it because they could get in and out of the river anytime they wanted, and could stay home by themselves when Nim, Jack, and Alex did things they didn't want to do. Nim, Jack, and Alex liked it because when they got back from a busy day in the busy city, they could breathe the fresh air and sit peacefully to watch the sun setting over the river and the buildings on the other side.

They went to museums and saw dinosaurs and tiny fossils, Egyptian mummies and suits of armor, enormous paintings and miniature carvings. They went to a library with paintings on the ceilings and stone lions outside the doors. They walked through the hot city streets and into chilled stores where women sprayed perfume that made Jack sneeze. They went to a movie theater and forgot to eat their popcorn because the screen was so big and the sound so all around them that they felt as if they were in the story too. They ate bagels and hot dogs and other foods Nim had never heard of; they had afternoon tea at the hotel that looked like a palace and rode through the streets in the carriage behind the horse called Mabel. They had a party with all their friends, with a special iguana-shaped cake that made Fred sneeze with surprise.

But best of all was the hot, hot day they all went to the huge park in the middle of the city. The taxi drove down a gently curving road and dropped them off where a path led to a tranquil green lake. When the driver opened the door, Selkie galumphed halfway down the path before he could even say "Here we are!"

"I didn't know they could move so fast!" said the driver.

Fred was racing behind Selkie as fast as his short iguana legs would carry him.

People jumped off the path out of their way, dogs barked— and Selkie and Fred slid into the water.

A row of turtles sunning on a log slowly turned their heads to stare and, one by one, disappeared under the water.

Fred came up from the bottom with a grin full of green plants.

Selkie popped up halfway across the lake to check if she could still see Nim. A gold tail stuck out of the side of her mouth.

Then, one by one, the dogs jumped in and paddled after Selkie and Fred, splashing and barking in the craziest, splashingest game of coconut-soccer-without-a-coconut that ever was.

Their families laughed as they watched them.

Other families wandering through the park came to watch.

And Nim, Alex, and Jack watched and laughed too, and sat on the bank together for the rest of the afternoon.

Postscript

To: erin@kidmail.com; ben@kidmail.com

From: nim@kidmail.com

Date: Thursday 2 August, 10:05 a.m.

Subject: Home on the island

Dear Erin and Ben,

I told you I'd write again as soon as we got back to the island. The city was so fun but I'm really happy I'm home now.

Our trip back was very different. This captain let Selkie and Fred have their own pool, and I slept in a cabin. It was a lot more comfortable, but I missed doing things with you. Once we saw a whale spouting and I wished you could have seen it too. We stopped at different places to take the smuggled animals back to their homes.

We bought a new sailboat when we got to Sunshine Island so we could sail the rest of the way. Jack was going to build our new boat but Alex said this was a present from her book, and Jack said okay because he wanted us all to be home again as fast as possible. Selkie swam most of the way, which was good because she took up all the deck when she had a nap; and also she liked showing the dolphins around, because they decided to follow us home. So did some of the birds.

Jack says the Professor and the Troppo captain should be in jail for a long, long time. I hope so. So do Kylie, Kelvin, and Kristie. They visited us at the houseboat and told us how upset they were when they found out about the animal smuggling. They're going to work on another boat now, and Virginia is going to work in a zoo to help animals who need to learn how to be free after being in cages for too long.

Did you see I have my own e-mail address now? So you can write to me as much as you want. But the best thing is that Jack and Alex said I can invite you to stay with us on the island next summer. I hope you'll come!
Love (as much as Selkie loves Fred),
Nim